Praise for *Heritage*

"*Heritage* is a lyrical fever dream of a novel. By turns tender and ferocious, meditative and searing, it traces a graceful, looping line across history and generations, in the process laying bare the shared dreams, joys, and traumas that connect us as human beings. I loved it."

—Jennifer Cody Epstein,
USA Today bestselling author of *Wunderland*

"Miguel Bonnefoy's *Heritage* shimmers off the page. The reader is seduced by three generations of the remarkable Lonsonier family, whose tales of anguish and love are echoed in the enchanting aviary they create in their garden in the Andes. The luminous characters endure passion and heartbreak through two world wars and beyond, with a plot that moves back and forth across continents. Translated exquisitely into English with beauty and precision, Bonnefoy's bold and magical book is a triumph."

—Patty Dann, author of *Mermaids* and *The Wright Sister*

"Mesmerizing and inventive, Miguel Bonnefoy's *Heritage* is a triumph alive with deeply felt characters braving new continents, wars, revolution, love, disillusion, ghosts, and even gravity as they strive to satisfy the simple yearnings of the heart against the cruelties of the human condition."

—Judithe Little, author of *The Chanel Sisters* and *Wickwythe Hall*

"In this bold and gripping saga, Miguel Bonnefoy intertwines his colorful characters' fates with those of their homelands, from Europe to the Americas. Mapuche traditions become laced with a legacy that is specific to the uprooted and a visceral attachment to a land that is at times welcoming, and at others, deadly, and whose sap is the blood of its inhabitants."

—*Lire*

"[Miguel Bonnefoy,] whose storytelling talent is consistently impressive, is a veritable prodigy... *Heritage* is already turning into one of the highlights of the fall season."

—*L'Express*

The Dream of the Jaguar

Also by Miguel Bonnefoy

Octavio's Journey

Black Sugar

Heritage

The Dream of the Jaguar

MIGUEL BONNEFOY

Translated from the French by Ruth Diver

Other Press
New York

First published in French in 2024 as *Le rêve du jaguar* by Éditions Payot & Rivages, Paris.

Production editor: Yvonne E. Cárdenas
Text designer: Patrice Sheridan
This book was set in Adobe Caslon by Alpha Design & Composition of Pittsfield, NH

10 9 8 7 6 5 4 3 2 1

Library of Congress Cataloging-in-Publication Data
Names: Bonnefoy, Miguel, 1986- author | Diver, Ruth translator
Title: The dream of the jaguar / Miguel Bonnefoy ; translated from the French by Ruth Diver.
Other titles: Rêve du jaguar. English
Description: New York : Other Press, 2025. | "First published in French in 2024 as Le rêve du jaguar by Éditions Payot & Rivages, Paris."— Title page verso.
Identifiers: LCCN 2025017157 (print) | LCCN 2025017158 (ebook) | ISBN 9781635425505 paperback | ISBN 9781635425512 ebook
Subjects: LCGFT: Fiction | Novels
Classification: LCC PQ2702.O556 R4813 2025 (print) | LCC PQ2702.O556 (ebook) | DDC 843/.92—dc23/eng/20250620
LC record available at https://lccn.loc.gov/2025017157
LC ebook record available at https://lccn.loc.gov/2025017158

Publisher's Note: This is a work of fiction. Names, characters, places, and incidents either are the product of the author's imagination or are used fictitiously, and any resemblance to actual persons, living or dead, events, or locales is entirely coincidental.

A la madre,
Y sonarán las campanas.

A Nene,
Al fín bailas.

“To the north is reason studying the rain,
deciphering the thunderclaps.
To the south are the dancers begetting the rain,
to the south are the drummers inventing the thunderclaps.”

—WILLIAM OSPINA

Antonio

On the third day of his life, Antonio Borjas Romero was abandoned on the steps of a church in a street that today bears his name. No one could be sure of the precise date on which he was found. All that is known is that every morning, a destitute woman would sit there, always in the same spot, put down a gourd bowl, and hold out her fragile hand to the passersby on the parvis. When she first set eyes on the infant, she pushed him away in disgust. But her attention was suddenly caught by a little shiny box hidden in the folds of his blanket, which someone had left with him as an offering: a tin rectangle, its silvery surface engraved with fine arabesques. It was a cigarette rolling machine. She filched it, put it into the pocket of her dress, then lost interest in the baby. But she noticed during the morning that the infant's timid wailing, his hesitant cries were so endearing to the churchgoers, who thought the two of them were together, that one by one they soon filled the bottom of her bowl with copper coins. When evening came, she took the baby to a farmyard, stuck his mouth to the teat of a black goat whose udder was covered in flies, and kneeled under its belly to make him suckle the thick warm milk. The next day, she wrapped him in a kitchen towel and hung him at her hip. After a week, she started saying that the child was hers.

This woman, whom everyone called Mute Teresa because she had a speech impediment, must have been somewhere in her forties, although she herself was incapable of giving her exact age. There was something Indian about her face, and on the left side, a slight paralysis caused by an ancient fit of jealousy. She carried nothing more than spongy skin on her bones, her hands were covered in sores that never healed, and her dirty white hair fell flat beside her face like the ears of a basset hound. She had lost the fingernail on her left thumb when a scorpion hiding in the back of a drawer had stung her hand one day. This did not kill her but formed a kind of sausage of flesh at the end of her thumb, a dead growth, and it was that flap that the child sucked before falling asleep during his first weeks.

She named him Antonio, for the church where she found him was placed under the patronage of Saint Anthony. She fed him with her own rage, with her silent pain. During his first few years, she had him lead a disorderly, shameful, indigent life. She convinced herself that if he should survive this misery, no one other than himself could kill him. At one year old, he could barely walk but could already beg. At two, he spoke sign language before he could speak Spanish. At three, he looked so much like her that she started wondering whether she had actually found him on the church steps, or might in fact have brought him into the world herself, in the backyard of a hovel, in the hollow of a hay bale, between a gray donkey and a lamb. She dressed him in filthy rags, and, to gain sympathy from the passersby, would hold him tight in fake tenderness, drenching him in acrid sweat that the heat turned into a kind of greasy yellow gelatin. She fed him goat cheese rolled by hand, slept with him in her shelter made of faded newspapers at the back of a makeshift sheep pen, and perhaps no woman ever showed so much courage in looking after a child she did not love.

Nevertheless, for Antonio, this lying, miserly, scurrilous, and thievish woman was the best possible mother to whom he could aspire. He took the roughness she showed him and the venomous love that poverty had woven between them to be tenderness. He grew up with her at La Rita, on the shores of Lake Maracaibo, in a place that was so dangerous that it was called Pela el Ojo, "Keep your eyes peeled."

When Antonio turned six, he no longer believed in miracles but sold jet pebbles as lucky charms and knew how to read cards, for Mute Teresa was adamant that this was the only science that people could be convinced by without it having the inconvenience of being true. When he turned eight, she taught him to recognize the crooked *aguadores*, the water carriers who sold dirty water from the lake passing it off as clean rainwater. But also the grocers who tipped their scales with a bent paper clip, the workmen who resold screws from the formwork on their building sites, and the trainers who, in the cockfighting pits, hid razor blades under the claws of the roosters' spurs. She had prepared him for this hard life, full of caution and necessity, of battles and suspicion, to the point that if a pastor suddenly announced during mass that a saint had burst into tears, Antonio was the first to raise his eyes to the church ceiling to see where the water leak was coming from.

In those days, Pela el Ojo was a kind of vast swamp crushed by the heat, with damp shores populated with little houses on stilts whose doors were always open. The dwellings were erected over that murky water, with open-air kitchens, blackened old stoves, and floating trash cans that the city had dumped on its outskirts. Bread was baked there, fuel was trafficked. The children lived naked on the boards, moving over this skeleton of thousands of tree trunks, which were constantly being patched up, wading on the surface of the lake as did the palaces in Venice, a sight which had made the Venetian navigators of long ago, arriving with their fragrances of vellum and sealing wax, say that they recognized it as a "little Venice," a *venezziola*, a Venezuela.

However, the immobility of these landscapes no longer conjured dreams of the ancient cities of the Caribbean, of Tamanaco and Mara, populated with women dressed in cotton gowns and mantles embroidered with gold, or young men whose chests were covered in fine silver dust, or newborn babies swaddled in jaguar skins. It was no longer a vision of a nation before all nations, of men dressed as eagles, of children who spoke with the dead and women who transformed themselves into salamanders.

At the time, it was no more than a township lacking in poetry, with roofs of hot palm fronds and teenagers wearing sandals cut out of old pickup-truck tires. The hovels were built from the hoods of old Indiana Trucks, the window handles from tin cans, the chair seats from aluminum posters for Shell. And since the rains were torrential and the palm-frond roofs needed to be protected, people bought old advertising billboards for Chevrolet, stolen at night along the highways, so that all the cladding of the shacks in the shantytowns, where people who could not drive slept, carried the words: "No happiness without Chevrolet."

Those rains, which were called *palo de agua*, often made the lake swell and burst its banks. The water flooded the plain in slow advances, drowning the countryside. The downpours could lash away continuously for forty furious nights, covering the fields with dead parrots, and when the tide reached the farms and submerged the crops, thousands of crayfish swam up from the gulf into the cornfields and enjoyed an underwater banquet that decimated the entire year's harvest in two weeks. People cursed the crayfish in Maracaibo as they cursed the grasshoppers in Egypt.

It was in this world that Antonio grew up, fishing on the lake, swimming through the pondweed and the mangroves. His diet was composed only of catfish, white-fleshed stone bass, blue crabs, and giant freshwater shrimp, to the point that Mute Teresa started to believe, in her most intrepid dreams, that Antonio would grow gills and start breathing underwater. One day when he was eleven years old, he put his hooks and lines into a bag, went to the village dock, and stole a canoe. Some children saw him and snitched on him. It did not take long for the owners of the vessel to appear in the distance. These were the rich men of La Rita, those who held power, those whose word was law on that side of the lake: Manu Moro, a tall fellow more than six foot seven, as wide at the waist as he was at the shoulders; Hermès Montero, an agitated little man who was red with anger; and Asdrubal Urribarri, a mixed-race man with green eyes and a clubfoot, wearing a white undershirt and waving his arms with a napkin in his hand, as if he had hastily stood up from the table.

"Antonio, I recognize you!" he shouted. "Come back here!"

On the shore, they were pacing furiously back and forth through the trash littering the beach, casting impetuous looks at Antonio as he paddled away. Asdrubal Urribarri disappeared, then came back again with a rabid dog with foaming jaws, which he threw into the water. The dog swam to the boat as if possessed and with an ease and energy that surprised everyone, climbed onto the boards and sprang at Antonio's neck. But Antonio had time to dodge it by jumping overboard and escaped by swimming against the current. The dog followed him, letting the boat float off to the horizon as Asdrubal yelled, "The boat! Don't let it get away!"

The dog persisted in its chase, barking feverishly, biting the waves, growling like mad. Antonio redoubled his efforts, dove underwater, and disappeared. After half an hour, when he felt a strong cramp pull at his thigh and his arms started stiffening with pain, he realized that the dog's barking had softened to whining, to the wails of the shipwrecked, and after a few minutes there was nothing but its little nose poking out of the water. It was only when the dog properly started to drown, yapping like a puppy, that Antonio decided to slow down. In a last gasp for survival, the dog caught up to him, and instead of biting him, eagerly clasped his shoulders. It was six in the evening. The owners of the boat, holding leather straps and belts, were watching keenly from the shore.

"You'll get tired in the end," they shouted. "We'll be waiting for you here."

Exhausted, with the dog on his back, Antonio let himself be carried by the current until he arrived at Punta Camacho, and resigned himself to waiting for darkness before getting out of the lake. Night fell only half a mile farther on, at Puerto Iguana, and when at last he was camouflaged by the light of the moon, protected by the darkness, he swam up to a little dock and ran, accompanied by the dog, toward the gates of Camino Real by the free pathway that led to Pela el Ojo.

As he was sighing with relief at the familiar sight of the lights of his hovel, reassured to have arrived home safe and sound at last, he got a sudden fright when he saw the silhouette of Asdrubal Urribarri, with his limping gait, talking to Mute Teresa, still waving his napkin and gesticulating wildly. Although Antonio was about to faint with exhaustion, he thought it was too dangerous to show himself. He found a solid palm tree, climbed up to the top, and waited for the night to be over.

The stars were enormous in the sky, and the world seemed flooded with silt. A group of men started tracking him. At the top of his palm tree, Antonio cried, not out of fear but out of rage. Alone and chilled by the wind from the lake, disturbed by the rustling of the fronds from which he had dislodged two rats nibbling at stalks in the crown, he took two hours to fall asleep while listening to the frogs copulating, and in his dreams he confused their croaking with men's voices.

He was awoken in the early morning by blows from a stick on his feet. He looked down to see Mute Teresa. She had searched for him all night in every shrub, in every sea grape tree along the shore, in vain. The dog, against all expectations and unbeknownst to its owner, had led her to him out of gratitude at having been saved from drowning. Mute Teresa put two cornmeal arepas and some grated cheese on a napkin on the ground. In her restricted language, she signaled for him to stay up in the tree for another night, maybe two, for Asdrubal Urribarri was keeping watch around their shelter. Antonio hunched over in anger.

"One day I will be a man, and I will no longer be afraid," he said from the top of the palm tree. "I'll teach him who's boss."

But Mute Teresa did not answer. Seeing him perched up there in that tree, hidden away and forgotten by everyone in the desolation of the world, she felt a pain in her soul, for she could conceive of no other future for Antonio than one as a street ruffian, born in the wrong place, dragging his loneliness until his death in the miserable rum joints where only vagrants and delinquents stray, desperate men who expect nothing from beauty and no longer know whom to die for. She imagined him as one of those brutes who was looking for him, who wanted to beat him, those nasty, arrogant men, raised on the lake's violence and by miserly fathers, whose hearts were thorns without a flower. Worse still, she imagined him like herself, living a life of disasters and frustrations, sitting on the steps of a church holding out a bony hand to strangers, ruminating on the humiliations and errors of her youth, having survived a childhood with no home nor refuge, with no love nor protection, a childhood when no one had taught her how to live.

That was the reason why, three days later, when everyone had forgotten the incident with the boat and Antonio was able to return home, Mute Teresa greeted him with patient gentleness. She was waiting for him there, perched on a little stool, doing her laundry, leaning over a tub, and when she saw him, so pale with hunger and exhaustion, trembling with fear and cold, she could not help wondering how humankind had managed to survive amid so much cruelty. She sat him on the ground in silence, took off his clothes, and gave him a summary wash in the laundry water, rubbing down his body, filling the tub with scraps of lake weed and palm bark, and they never said so much as a word about this incident for the rest of their lives.

The next day, she searched the recesses of her hovel and put a package into his hands. Antonio, who had never received a present before, opened it quickly. It was the little cigarette rolling machine she had found, eleven years earlier on the church steps, in the folds of his blanket. These letters were engraved on the back: Borjas Romero. She looked Antonio straight in the eye, and it was one of the rare occasions he heard her voice.

"If you want to become the boss, don't steal," she muttered. "Work."

And so Antonio got it into his head to sell cigarettes. He got his first handful of tobacco thanks to his cunning. One September morning, a few days after the episode with the boat, he crossed the only square in La Rita and with a determined step entered the La Pioja grocery store belonging to Henri Reille, a fine fellow in his forties with no shady dealings, full of health and vitality, the son of immigrants from Nantes who had come at the beginning of the century and whose French lineage had endowed him with the bold art of commerce. Antonio offered him the following deal: "Give me some tobacco and some paper. I'll come back this evening with double its price."

Antonio left Henri Reille with ten grams of tobacco, rolled thirty cigarettes, and went to the port of Santa Rita, where dozens of men arrived every day from the south of Lake Maracaibo, the mountains of Mérida, and the backwaters of Santander, Trujillo, and Táchira, disembarking on the dock from their dinghies hewn from a single tree trunk and canoes filled with animals whose cries echoed throughout the bay. He sold everything he had until nightfall, handling his machine as if it were a Venetian lute and calculating each gram of tobacco with the care of a goldsmith, economizing each sliver of paper. At around seven, he returned to the grocery store and set down the bounty of the day on the counter, under Henri Reille's astonished eyes.

"You are richer this evening than you were this morning," he said. "And so am I. Let's keep going."

For three weeks, in the suffocating heat of the coast, he went tirelessly back and forth from Pela el Ojo to La Rita, persuading anyone he crossed paths with on the port to have a smoke. With savage obstinacy, he mingled with the vast community of sellers of crushed ice and *guarapo*, the cold drink made from sap, sugar paste, and pinole, until the day when a goods porter offered him three pennies to help him unload some sacks of coconuts from a boat.

Antonio, who at that age already had wide shoulders and a muscular back, threw one of the sacks onto his spine with the help of two leather straps, surprised himself with the strength of his arms and the solidity of his legs, then hunched forward and walked off under the weight toward the truck, with a blind tenacity that the other porters ascribed not to his strength but to his youth. Despite the excessive weight that compressed his lungs, he managed to unload everything, and earned in one hour with his arms what it would have taken all day to earn with his cigarettes. From that day onward, he never set foot in Henri Reille's grocery store again. The following day, he came back to the same spot on the dock, convinced that he would make a fortune with the strength of his muscles, but he quickly understood that there was a hierarchy in all things, even in the world of porters.

He was introduced to an old boatman called Alfaro who was in need of laborers, a hawk-nosed man from Panama whose fingers were covered in rings and was notorious for his abrupt mood swings and choleric character. Antonio was a model of discipline and flexibility, uncomplaining, obedient, and selfless. He was happy to do whatever was assigned to him. In the stifling air of the port, where the docks were covered every day with crates of fragrant spices and cages of flowers, Antonio learned to read, to count, to recognize the maritime flags that the smugglers modified to thwart the coast guard, to calculate by touch alone the worth of the coins he was given, and to file away in his imagination not only all the accents he heard around him but also all the fabulous stories that came to him with the arriving goods and that blended together in his head as in a great ancient novel.

This is how he learned of the existence, in the south, of a village that moved around, a shifting village that gravitated around Barinas as a planet around a star, and that could only be found by chance. He heard about the legend of the solid-gold Virgin of Benito Bonito, about the opera house in Manaus built in the middle of the jungle, about the thirty-eight-minute-long war in Zanzibar and the story of an Andalusian settler who brought four hundred elephants from Nepal to fill his stables in the middle of a desert in the dunes of Coro. These marvelous tales remained etched so profoundly in the marble of his memory that, many years later, when the plaque was unveiled in the street that bore his name, Antonio was able to relive with acute precision that stifling morning in the little port of Santa Rita when all at once, in the middle of the tumult of ropes and heavy chains, he saw the statue of the *libertador* Simón Bolívar arrive at its port of call in Maracaibo.

It loomed up one Tuesday in November. The lake dwellers saw it in the distance, on the promenade covered in crushed mangoes and rotten fish, an imposing statue four yards high made from six tons of bronze cast in Tuscany. It was of a man on horseback in nineteenth-century dress, looking straight ahead and pointing his sword at the future with an authoritarian air. His elegance was so striking to the children on the beach, boys in rags who had never seen Simón Bolívar, that they ran into their shacks yelling, "God has come down to Maracaibo!" After a perilous traction with iron pulleys, weights, and straps, Simón Bolívar was unloaded from the ship and set down between the chicken cages and crates of plantains and dried meat, surrounded by sacks of coffee. The bronze stank of guavas. The statue had come a long way, having made a voyage on the ship down the course of a tumultuous river and survived rust and oxidation as well as the tropical rainstorms that had broken out several times and fifty miles of crocodiles and howler monkeys. It was supposed to stay a few days in Maracaibo before continuing its journey up the Rio Escalante to reach the port of Santa Bárbara del Zulia, across from the city of San Carlos where, one day in 1820, Simón Bolívar, making the most of the abundance of wood in the area, had ordered the construction of five ships to attack the Spanish.

By two o'clock, the whole town had heard about the visit of the *libertador*. People were crowding around the statue in a carnival of acclamation, carrying children on their shoulders and bringing the elderly out of their rooms to see it, and there were even some Guajiro on the dock, who had come down barefoot from the Sierra de Perijá with birds in their hands and a ruckus of tiny bells, attracted by the rumor that a metal man had been discovered in the middle of their lake. It was not long before the local authorities made an official appearance, with the governor of the province of Zulia at their head, along with other town dignitaries, to render homage to the hero of the nation, by trampling the jumble of rotten fruit.

Eventually the speeches were so long and pompous that, over the course of the ten days that the statue was standing by on the port of Maracaibo, people ended up losing their curiosity. At night, some men who were roaming around the docks tried to paint the horse's rump, while others threw avocados as big as melons at the *libertador*'s head, and still others tried to steal his sword by cutting it with a lumber saw, but they managed only to leave a notch an inch deep in the palm of his hand, such that three days later, when the statue was examined, this was believed to be the mysterious trace of a Christlike stigmata.

An unexpected incident, deceptive because it masked another, forced Antonio to change trades once again. After the departure of Simón Bolívar, the old boatman Alfaro woke up suddenly in the middle of the night because of a huge racket outside. He could no longer feel his legs. Pins and needles ran all over his arms, he started suffocating and died a few minutes later without having had time to call for help. Although he was advanced in years, it was not old age that had killed him but a heart attack at 4:30 a.m. at home in his own bed, on the day of El Reventón, when the workers of the Venezuelan Oil Concession company discovered the first petroleum deposit that would soon overturn the entire economy of the country.

It was at Cabimas that the explosion was first heard. Everyone was startled when a thunderclap made the latches on the shutters jump and opened all the windows in the neighborhood in a single blast. According to the press, the residents thought it was a tree uprooted by lightning that had fallen on an old hacienda in a powerful storm, and when they came out into the street, they discovered to their stupefaction that it was not raining water but a black viscous liquid. Beyond the Barrosos' family house, in the sky in the distance, a dark column could be seen rising like the tower of a cursed castle, forty yards high, an inexhaustible geyser constantly growling and spitting rocks into the sky.

"Oil! Oil!" the workers yelled.

Samuel Smith, the engineer from the United States who was in charge of the Venezuelan Oil Concession, a man with gray eyes and a Greek nose, was awoken in the early hours of the morning by the same thunderclap that killed Alfaro the boatman. He gave orders for the auger to be removed immediately to stop the flow, but by then the stream was running over several yards between the rocks and the coconut palms, snaking toward the lake. At dawn, the crown was broken by the rocks and the stream had become a sticky river. By midday, the accumulated sand had reached the metallic gates surrounding the grounds of the well, and no valve, not even the one brought from Punta de Leiva on a tractor borrowed from a farmer in Cabimas, could contain the gusher. That evening, Samuel Smith, who was living a nightmare, had to resign himself to using the hoses of a drill that the company owned on the Río El Limón and to installing two pumps across from La Rosa to carry away the spilled oil.

But the black flood was unstoppable. It rained oil for nine days nonstop. It was said that that first well let one hundred thousand barrels escape daily without being brought under control, one hundred thousand barrels of oil that had to be discarded, for no one knew how to refine it. And the well would have continued to gush for another twenty years if not for the appearance one morning, when all was thought to be lost, of a certain Andrés Arrieta, a devotee of San Benito de Palermo, the Black saint, who marched into Samuel Smith's office and asked to talk to him.

Andrés Arrieta was a Creole of medium height. With his lively eyes and white linen robes, he looked like one of those alchemists of the Middle Ages who tried to discover the secret magical properties of metals. Although he was bald, he wore colored bands on his head that seemed to hold back an imaginary mane of hair, and he had embroidered scapulars on his chest, fishing twine around his wrists, and spots of wax on his hands.

"Give us access to the well," said Arrieta. "San Benito will stop the gusher."

His voice had a soft firmness. Samuel Smith stared at him with his wide gray eyes and burst out laughing.

"If you go in there, no one will come out alive, not you nor your saint."

"San Benito will protect us," he replied.

Andrés Arrieta insisted so much that he was granted access to the well. He went away to bring out the saint from a chapel in La Rita, then returned accompanied by eight mixed-race men with coppery skin carrying drums held by straps around their necks and concealing their faces behind masks of devils. As they held up San Benito on a litter, they entered the enclosed grounds of the well with great pomp, chanting African litanies as they crossed El Cardonal under a shower of black rain. As the noisy procession was heading to the center of the drill site, convinced that only a miracle would be able to stop the flow, they started bathing San Benito in the oil to the rhythm of the percussions. Other men mingled into the throng, dancers and ritual singers, brandishing fans and whips, raising the crosses of various parishes, when all at once the gusher stopped dead.

Samuel Smith was so struck by this prodigious coincidence that many years later, in the living room of his house in Boconó, in the state of Trujillo, where he was living with his second wife, he still wondered whether this scene had not been a mystical dream. But he had no need to force his memory to recall with accuracy the enormous public holiday that the Venezuelan Oil Concession had organized for the *sanbeniteros*, in front of Abraham Perozo's store, and how that evening, after experiencing one of the strangest encounters between magic and science, he had decided to become a devotee of San Benito until the end of his days.

As soon as the gusher from the well was contained, three hundred men were brought from Carora and the Andes to build a wall as thick as a dam to stem the flow and stop the oil from reaching the lake. Antonio was one of those men. Working from one Monday to the next, carrying sandbags and pushing wheelbarrows of cement, living in the laborers' dormitories where, alongside the line of tents, thousands of picked flowers wilted in carts, he barely had time to have a childhood. He quickly turned into a vigorous adolescent, made strong by arduous labor. His voice broke into deeper, more assured tones, his hands became veined, his chin was covered with his first beard hairs, and his arms grew to the size of a galley slave's.

Everything in him was fecundity, robustness, joy. It took no effort at all for him to lift the heavy loads, to cover walls in whitewash, to hide his exhaustion. A pulsating vitality flowed through him. And he was so focused on his work that he did not notice the metamorphosis of his own body, nor the speed with which the area was being populated by foreigners and migrants. For the rumor of a new promised land had spread like wildfire and no one could ignore any longer the fact that Lake Maracaibo was now a gold mine.

The discovery of oil changed everything. The town was transformed at the same time as Antonio. With the massive arrivals of convoys of eager men, what had been just a village of fishermen and gleaners only a few months earlier became a Babel-like city that sprang up in a single night.

All of Maracaibo was stunned by the spectacle of the trucks parked in long mute lines on the outskirts of town, loaded with men coming from the most faraway regions of Tucupita, the valleys of the Orinoco delta, and the ethereal depths of the Gran Sabana. In the port, dozens of bulk freighters that no one had ever seen before arrived daily, flying the flags of the United States, Great Britain, or Korea, with heavy cargoes of businessmen and suitcases of dollars. Then more foreigners appeared, exhausted Gypsies who knew how to predict the sky's vagaries by measuring the thickness of sap, Dutchmen and Italians who had taken any ship they could find and had the names of prostitutes tattooed on their chests, Arabs and *garimpeiros* in military uniforms coming out of the jungle, Chilean winegrowers who had climbed up the cordillera on foot in the hope of finding new land. All these men were suddenly there, on that lakeshore covered in coal tar and camellias, on a quest to find black gold.

Within a few days, Antonio heard cussing in all the languages of the globe and learned more about the world than in the previous twelve years of his life. Bubbling, exalted, dazzling, the town metamorphosed so abruptly, so completely, that it seemed the whole world had moved there, and the houses were crowded with so many residents that beds needed to be imported from Caracas by an exceptional convoy commanded by the governor himself, for people had already started confiscating the mattresses from the hospitals and the bunks from the barracks. A crowd of women of easy virtue invaded the cafés, the outdoor tables of the restaurants, the canteens and sidewalks of the Avenida del Milagro. The streets were bustling with legions of beggars and adventurers, ruffians and skinflints, gold diggers and scrooges from all the prisons and cabarets of the Americas, and never had this little village on the shores of a forgotten gulf seen so many visitors since the day, four centuries earlier, when the German Ambrosius Ehinger had landed on these shores, accompanied by one hundred soldiers, to found what he believed was a land of God.

Antonio left Santa Rita more or less in this period. One of the oldest workmen on the Venezuelan Oil Concession's wall, Atilio Berenice, an albino who must have been a hundred and fifty but seemed no older than thirty because of his immutable strength, told him about a brothel looking for a jack-of-all-trades.

"It's called the Majestic. Tell them you've come from me."

Antonio went there that very evening. The Majestic was a meeting place on the other side of the lake, far away from everything, next to an outgrowth of the city made up of miserable stinking alleyways of beaten earth, where children lived naked and men died without ever having been loved. On a wooden sign painted in red on the facade, the word *Majestic* appeared in shining letters, in calligraphy that recalled the elongated signatures of the first governors of the province of Zulia.

It was an old four-story house, regal and large, probably once belonging to a settler in the service of Castile, so vast that after two days of cleaning, when the last room was finished, the dust had already settled again in the first one. That Sisyphean task was carried out with no rest or interruption in that shadowy kingdom, where the rooms were lined with cork to stifle the excesses of passion and furnished with pieces from the tropical junk stores, blue marble statues of the Virgin, paintings of fishermen coming home from the sea, alabaster allegories holding cornucopias, a harp with golden arabesques that no one had ever played, and mirrors with mannered baroque frames on all the walls, as in a crystal museum, before which the young ladies would take turns rearranging their hair with seductive gestures.

Antonio knocked on the front door. When he was asked who he was, he mentioned Atilio Berenice's name.

"Wait here," answered a woman's voice.

The main door finally opened. He crossed a long corridor leading to a room with padded walls. In that salon, under a lace lampshade beside an Arabian side table, a woman was sitting with a cigar in her hand. Her name was known throughout the town: Lucrecia Montilla. She wore a flower with tiger-striped petals tucked behind her ear, flat chain-link bracelets around her wrists, and a cascade of mixed perfumes.

"How old are you?"

"Thirteen," Antonio lied.

She raised her arm, covered in bracelets and gold bands, and motioned for him to approach. When he was standing next to her, she suddenly put her hand between his legs.

She smiled. "You seem younger."

She must have once been an arrogant beauty, and the traces of her good looks could still be discerned under her bestial wrinkles, but at present her large awkward body was built of hard, compact clay so heavy that she could only sit down with the help of two people. Her hands smelled of rice powder, cinnamon blush, nail polish, false eyelashes, pomegranate-colored rhinestones, hair-removal wax, and local corruption.

"What do you know how to do?" she asked.

"Everything," Antonio replied.

Some girls lying on the floor giggled. They were the youngest in the house. Their long, glossy, scented hair blended into the patterns in the carpet to create what looked like a roomful of snakes. Lucrecia Montilla looked him over from head to toe and seemed satisfied.

"Come back in three days then," she said. "Here everything needs doing."

Three days later, Antonio arrived punctually at nine in the morning, as agreed. When he pushed open the door of the Majestic, it took him a while to get over his astonishment when he saw, in the middle of the room, a mountain of cut hair, piled up like a haystack. This auburn hill had kept a few scarlet highlights and must have weighed almost four pounds. Next to it he saw a figure dressed in a white alpaca robe sitting in a corner on a velvet chair, who appeared to him to be a faun sculpted out of alabaster.

It was a girl with a shaved head who was having her scalp massaged with macadamia oil by two Indian women. She was gazing into the void. Her skin was pale. Antonio thought she might be twenty, but there was something in the way she sat, a kind of despondency and exhaustion, something in the prominent veins on her hands and the sadness on her forehead that made him think she might be twice that age. She appeared to be frozen, immobile, like a statue lost in a world of which he knew nothing, and Antonio suspected from the terrifying expression in her eyes that in this isolated brothel all the crimes of passion were committed with perfect impunity.

This girl was called Leona Coralina. She had arrived in Maracaibo from across the Colombian border, after hearing that it was raining oil on the other side of the mountains, and also fleeing the coercion of a pimp with long blond mustaches, a man riddled with vices who had promenaded her along all the sidewalks of Cartagena in silk stockings, and delivered her to cohorts of tourists for a crust of bread. One February evening, finally accepting that she was the only one who could change her destiny, she cut off her hair and sold it to pay for the guides in the sierra so she could cross the border, following paths through the impenetrable jungle, going on a long and dangerous journey with fuel smugglers who wanted to be paid in kind, and finally reached the port of Maracaibo with a short bob and an extra ten years.

When she arrived, she started working for Lucrecia Montilla at the Majestic, for she had the misfortune of not knowing how to do anything else. But against all expectations, this new departure, although tiresome, offered her a second youth. One morning, she noticed with astonishment that her dark brown hair had grown back a different color during her perilous jungle crossing, and that she now had flaming, triumphant, blood-red hair, which she ascribed to a miracle conceded only to girls who had been through hell.

According to legend, two hours were required to look after this Dantesque mane, which tumbled to her hips in velvety drapery, its tresses decorated in braids in the fashion of the Margarita saleswomen, whose curls were so famous in the town that they were said to have curative properties. The rumor spread rapidly. Sailors would come knocking at the door of the Majestic to spend an hour with Leona, just so they could confirm the veracity of the stories for themselves, and they would leave for their seas of misfortune making the sign of the cross on the threshold, convinced that from that day forward they were blessed by her locks. In the thick night of Maracaibo, from the entrance foyer, you could see lines of men smelling of eau de cologne, hiding their banknotes in their long johns, speaking all the languages of the world, wearing talismans made of albatross feathers around their necks to protect them from shipwreck, moving forward in a great pilgrimage toward her room, each one coming to purge his soul on the same pillow.

Two weeks later, the news reached the ears of the governor himself, who made a secret appearance one evening, disguised as a sailor, and declared that he would hand over the deeds to the property if he was allowed to ejaculate in her hair. News of the visit spread through the house and Lucrecia Montilla, a cunning and greedy woman who was accustomed to men's whims, entered Leona's room and asked her in an assured voice what she thought of this.

Leona observed her with a vacant expression. "I will accept only under one condition."

"And what might that be?"

"That I get my head shaved afterward."

It was at that time that Antonio arrived at the Majestic. The first thing he was asked to do was to pick up Leona's hair, which had taken up so much space in the main room of the house that it took two wheelbarrows to carry it all away, leaving behind a fragrance of equatorial roses.

He was hired to do odd jobs: changing sheets, scrubbing pots, mopping the tile floor, sweeping the bedrooms, cleaning, polishing, scouring the sinks, making coffee, and lighting twelve Coleman oil lamps, which needed to be handled with care or the whole house could explode. Since he was the only man employed in the establishment, he was soon nicknamed El Hombrecito. He was given a tiny room that, compared to the cardboard box where he had spent his childhood, seemed to him to be the great hall of a castle. The ceiling was so narrow, the walls so close that it was impossible to install a rotary fan in there. The hundred-year-old beams, hewn from the timber of a ship salvaged from the days of Henry Morgan, were still redolent of the foam of sea voyages and the pipe smoke of buccaneers, such that at certain times of the day, the heat made their wooden pores exude the salty smell of ancient piracy.

Once a week, Lucrecia Montilla would subject her girls to a hygiene examination that omitted nothing. It was she who instructed them in the art of seduction, who groomed them according to the latest practices in love, and imposed on them an alacrity and lightness that had not been seen since the bordellos of Pompeii.

According to the legend of the Majestic, all the girls were descendants of the same man, Ambrosius Ehinger, a doughty German who had arrived at La Barra four hundred years ago with two brigantines and a caravel filled with cannons, and who had disembarked in that lost corner of the world with a hundred soldiers and forty horses. It was said that he first had a parish church built with a palm-frond roof and earth-brick walls in the spot where there once had been a small Indigenous community composed of a few isolated huts, which everyone called Maracaibo.

Driven mad by incurable gold fever, he had attacked the neighboring villages looking for the city of emeralds and pearls, had slashed earlobes to steal earrings, nostrils to take nose rings, feet for ankle bracelets, and heads for necklaces. He had filled studded coffers in Germany with diadems covered in blood and thanked God, had raped all the women of the hamlets he pillaged, and, before dying pierced with fifteen arrows by the warriors of Pamplona, had found the time to give the world fifty girls as blond as amber, fifty danaids with covellite eyes whose great-great-granddaughters would end up in that tropical house of ill repute, paying the price of that ancient malediction.

Antonio lived there for two years. Every morning, Lucrecia Montilla would administer to him a potion made of bromide and white waterlilies, reputed to reduce sexual appetite, in order to ensure that the afternoon's chores would be completed without the interference of desire. At the end of the day, when the concoction had lost its potency, Antonio could feel the urges stifled by the plants rise up inside him, and the wild essence of his lust would take over once again. He was usually sent to bed before the arrival of the first customers. But at night the brothel made so much noise that Antonio had no need to stick his ear to the walls to imagine the wondrous contortions that the girls of the Majestic performed. All it took was an ungreased spring, the scratch of nails on a dresser, a laugh, or a moan for him to have no trouble imagining the scene that was taking place a few yards from him. For hours, the clandestine loves of Lake Maracaibo flooded his little servant's room with the force of a deluge, and when he fell asleep at last in the hubbub of voices and window shutters, of mirrors and swishing skirts, his dreams were only of shipwrecked nymphs with mahogany skin.

In March, the Majestic was populated with young women from foreign parts, who had come from all four corners of the earth, attracted by the crowds of solitary men inspired by the discovery of oil. The girls seemed not so much to have come from another continent as to belong to a different species altogether. Their fragrances from unknowable climes would leave the sailors of Maracaibo with a lasting heady imprint of distant mythologies.

Every morning at ten, as they floated around the house in scanty attire, chattering about the whims of the previous night's customers, Antonio would notice the constellations of marks left by men's fingers on the whiteness of their backs and the discreet bruises on their knees, affixed like two silver seals, which showed the relentless devotion with which they had communed all night long.

Kindled by these comings and goings, he would contemplate in silence the nipples fortuitously popping out of their blouses, the lascivious backbends, and the stretch marks striping their round buttocks. Antonio was entering an age when it was no longer so simple to resist desire. But the girls of the Majestic were still amused by his natural timidity with an almost maternal detachment. He remained in their eyes only El Hombrecito. None of them shared the fascination that he secretly projected onto them in his fiery desire, and it was impossible for him to find inner peace, until one day at the end of May a miraculous accident came to cure him of that heavy solitude and initiated him to the largesse of maturity.

The third Thursday of the month, Antonio became a man. At that time, he was in charge of changing the week's dirty sheets, which were green with sweat, and of bringing them to El Pedrazo laundry, for Lucrecia Montilla had decreed that the stains could only be masked by herring brine. One stifling hot morning, after a bacchanalian night when half the town had visited the brothel, Antonio entered one of the rooms to strip the bed and surprised Leona Coralina stretched out on the mattress with her generous form like that of a sea lion sleeping on a rock, dressed only in a long string of pearls looped several times around her neck.

Ten men had passed through this room during the night, and a strong odor of saliva and sweat still emanated from the walls. She had her buttocks turned toward the door, her head lying on a towel she had rolled into a ball, and her body was barely covered by a thin blue linen sheet from which one enormous breast was escaping, still red from its recent passions and with purple veins so prominent that her fortune could be read there with more accuracy than in the palm of her hand.

Antonio, who was by now accustomed to feminine nudity, tiptoed out and shut the door softly. He was about to enter the next room when a hand pulled him abruptly backward. He found himself face-to-face with Leona. She had stood up and caught him. She threw him onto the bed without a word, tore off his pants that were held up only with a canoe rope, tied his hands to the bars of the bedstead, climbed on top of him, then gave him such satisfaction, such ecstasy, with such marvelous skill gained from her long experience, that Antonio wondered what the unknowable diamonds were that graced women's insides. He never forgot that exquisite pleasure, that astonishing fervor, and when he later thought back to that morning, all that he could recall was an intense memory of ships loaded with centaurs and cinnamon.

The next day, Leona's exceptional curves haunted his thoughts with the savage power of an epiphany. The image of that nudity never left him. His desire to see her again was so obsessive he could think of nothing else during his housework. That body which had touched his was the body of all bodies, it was the mythical body of the empress of the Amazons, the body that the adventurers of the conquest had deliriously searched for in vain, throughout the distant depths of the Oriental and Occidental Indies, the body which had by now been removed to the body of this exiled Colombian woman, selling her heart for a few pesos in a miserable room in the Caribbean. He had never known a woman whose memory had provoked such intrepid fantasies, whose forms left him nostalgic and with so little peace, and there was no valley in the world large enough to hold the rivers of love that Antonio poured forth in his imagination.

One morning a week later, he could stand it no longer and entered her room again while she was sleeping. Seeing her naked like the first time, he undressed in silence but, at the moment when he slipped under the sheets, she turned her head over her shoulder and said, with the tender voice of those who know the wounds of virility, "The first time was free, *mi amor.* Now that you're a man, you'll have to pay like everyone else."

It was during this period that the men from the north started arriving. Six months earlier, the news that a company was seeking to hire laborers to extract oil from the mountains of Perijá had spread to all the café tables on Plaza Baralt, to all the surrounding villages, along the whole coast of Sinamaica, and it did not take long for giants with long blond beards and aluminum helmets to appear on the dock, carrying pipes and leaping onto trucks in the alleyways sprayed with black oil.

In the evenings, their bellies full of aguardiente and their heads emptied by the roar of the drills, they would head for the lit-up signs, seeking to spend what remained of their hard-earned pittance on their appetite for women with exotic names. Tall and strong, they had miraculously survived malaria and snakebites during their exodus, and at night they loved to get into diabolical fights, making the chairs fly and the bottles explode against the walls, such that it was not rare to find gold coins in foreign currencies fallen from their pockets under the tables the next morning, a hint of what would happen in Venezuela in the century to come.

These brawls, which often occurred around 2:00 a.m. and shook the whole house, incited Lucrecia Montilla to hire a doorman to screen the customers, as well as a cleaning lady. One day, without providing any explanation whatsoever, she went to find Antonio in his little room. Confounded by this unusual visit, he welcomed her with suspicion, but Lucrecia announced that the arrival of these two new staff members would henceforth change the order of the household.

"Your position has just improved," she told him.

From that day forward, Antonio no longer had to light the Coleman lanterns, nor change the sheets, nor mop the floors, nor even drink the bromide potion that she concocted for him every morning. He was promoted to the bar. She increased his salary.

At fourteen, he was already tall, with broad shoulders and a narrow forehead, and had that expression of natural authority that would make him famous during the days of the dictatorship. To make his presence more impressive, Lucrecia Montilla had him wear white shirts, starched so that the collar would stay stiff all night, and forbade him to drink water from the tap to avoid the dangers of cholera.

Antonio was thus allowed to drink only ginger beer and to always have a packet of Chesterfield cigarettes in his shirt pocket. He would slip behind the bar every evening, and during his shift, which lasted until 3:00 a.m., he would listen to the stories told by the drunks and bachelors who had traveled all over the world and come to find consolation in their solitude with girls smelling of white brambles. He met the sculptor Carmelo Fernández, accompanied by an obese woman with breasts so big that she could have fed a stable of young bulls, who told him about how he had unbolted the plaque of General Venancio Pulgar, which he had made himself, on the day when the people came down into Plaza Bolívar to shout his name. He met Marc-Étienne Sainte-Musse, a Haitian from Port-au-Prince, who was nicknamed The Nose, and who had been one of the first to use the technique of enfleurage of violets on the islands and to create essential oils from black currants, until the day when he lost his legendary sense of smell by contracting a venereal disease on a ship off the coast of Brazil. He met a man called Narciso Morocota who answered only to the name Piano Leg, a lame gardener from Plaza Baralt thus baptized because he wore a shoe with an iron point that clanked on the ground as he walked.

Until dawn, all the picturesque characters of Maracaibo in the 1930s would pass through the vapors of Irish whiskey in the bar: the one called Culebrita, because he had a wooden hut next to a flea market where he sold rum made from grass snakes which could wake the devil; Benoît Bramont, a French workman, as solid as an ox, who had arrived by chance in Venezuela after a drunken night in Paris, and who sold curious solar machines and declared he was the disciple of a certain Augustin Mouchot, an inventor no one had heard of; Carlos Luis Rosales, a coachman in the plaza, who had built the first hot-air balloon in the Caribbean out of cardboard and canvas, and successfully flew over the lake twice but on the third attempt was found drowned by boatmen from Lagunillas, his belly swollen by a foam of blue flowers. And maybe Antonio would have continued listening to these interminable stories for many years more, were it not for the appearance, the evening of the first of November, of an extravagant sailor dressed in a taffeta suit with a pattern of dragons and a scent of crinolines, holding a leather briefcase monogrammed E.B.R. under his arm, who introduced himself as Elías.

He was the captain of his own ship, *El Nautilus*. He would regularly stop off at Ceuta del Agua, at Moporo, at La Dificultad, and at other ports on the south side of the lake. He loved to sing Cuban boleros. Antonio saw him as he was talking at the back of the room, making elegant gestures with his arms, in the middle of a circle of girls. His body was slumped on Moroccan poufs, almost reclining, his hair was thick, and his tiny teeth, one of which was solid gold, were all bunched together and worn away by forty years of tobacco. It was the tone of his voice that first attracted Antonio's attention. A high-pitched, harmonious, soft voice, such as one might use when talking to children, which was in stark contrast to the place, and which aroused a perverse curiosity in the women. He looked like a mixture of a Sevillian Gypsy and an English gentleman, with an air that was both untamed and refined, and vaguely reminded Antonio of the profile of the *libertador*, which he had seen a few years previously on the bronze statue when it had disembarked one day on the docks of Santa Rita.

Cheerful, comical, and garrulous, he gestured for Antonio to approach and asked for a light for his cigarette. His head was full of anecdotes heard during his travels. He knew the melody of the winds, the language of the tides, and from so many voyages on board *El Nautilus* over so many years along the entire coast, he had ended up learning the rumors of all the ports, of all the villages that marked his circuit from Concepción to the wild palm trees of Bobures, such that he knew everyone by their first name, even those he had never met. And while he was downing glasses of Old Parr with a girl on his knee and talking about the day when the president Juan Vicente Gómez was his passenger, he unbuttoned his waistcoat with the gold dragons and brought out a little box. Inside was a cigarette rolling machine. A tin rectangle, its silvery surface engraved with fine arabesques. The device was so similar to Antonio's that he could not help crying out: "That's funny!"

"What's funny?" asked the sailor as he licked the paper.

And so Antonio brought out his own machine and showed it to him. The sailor stopped what he was doing and his eyes filled with tears. He was suddenly sad, as if struck by guilt. He seemed ashamed of himself and sent away the girl who was sitting on his knee. With no explanation, he paid for his glass, turned his back on Antonio, and disappeared.

A few weeks later, he came back strung with African necklaces. He had just returned from a tiresome voyage from Santa Apolonia with disciples of the cult of María Lionza, led by Babel Bracamonte, a tall ageless Indian man descended from a legendary family of gold miners and workmen, a black magic sorcerer, who had gone in search of cowries and other shells in the caves of Chivacoa. On the fifth day of the crossing, Babel Bracamonte had made him drink liquor made from tapir blood and had smoked him with black tobacco, the effects of which were to transport Elías on a long internal journey.

He had gone back to the origins of his childhood. He had revisited all the stages of his life, from the day when two identical cigarette rolling machines were made in front of his eyes, to the tragic morning when, having just buried his wife, frightened and alone, he had abandoned his only child on the steps of a church, hiding one of the machines in the folds of his blanket. Antonio, who knew nothing of this whole story, did not have time to serve him another drink, for the sailor brought out of his bag a piece of paper folded in four and slid it over to him on the bar. This man who was usually so lighthearted did this with conspiratorial gravity, as if it were a kind of pact, and Antonio tucked the letter into his pocket, staring at him in silence with an expression of distrust mixed with curiosity, never suspecting that he was thus accepting a mute oath of trust that would endure until his dying day.

This letter was addressed to a certain Victor Emiro Montero, who was Elías's brother. It was composed with the hesitant effort of those who have lost the habit of writing. As he read it in his little room with the close-set rafters, Antonio learned that, for an enigmatic reason that remained unknown to him for many years, the sailor was asking Don Victor Emiro to receive Antonio well, to offer him a respectable home, and to enroll him at school. Attached to the letter was a bundle of banknotes for his expenses, without any additional explanation. Antonio waited for two months for Elías to return to unravel the mystery, but he could never gather any more information, neither on the brother nor on the identity of that tormented mariner, for Elías never set foot in the Majestic again.

Under different circumstances, Antonio might have stolen the money, scrunched up the letter, and thrown it into the nearest trash can in the bar. But it had arrived at precisely the moment in his life when he was starting to tire of the Majestic and its constant traffic of drunkards and battlers, of women of loose morals and disguised cops, where there was only insidious pettiness, venal jealousy, and calculated seduction. He decided to take the risk. Before midday, he dressed in his only linen jacket, put on his raffia espadrilles, and smoothed brilliantine on his hair. With the same courage he had displayed to get as far as he already had, from that afternoon when Atilio Berenice had told him about this brothel, Antonio pressed the letter into the lining of his jacket and went into Lucrecia Montilla's room. She was both surprised and disconcerted to see him, mainly because it was the first time he had ever knocked at her door, but also because she thought he was happy with his raise.

"I have come to announce my departure from the Majestic," he said with determination.

It was not so much the words themselves that troubled Lucrecia Montilla as the conviction with which they were spoken. She hardly recognized, in the cool-headed, self-possessed young man standing before her with his linen jacket and fashionable hairstyle, the docile, trembling child she had opened the door of her establishment to a mere two years ago. Faced with his stubbornness, she understood that it would be pointless to try to retain him, but her old vixen's instinct compelled her to try one last time. She raised her arm, covered in bracelets and gold bands, and motioned for him to approach. Antonio did not let himself get caught again.

"Not this time," he said.

Lucrecia Montilla burst out laughing. "How old are you?"

"Fourteen."

"You seem older, *hombrecito*. Now, get out of here. I never want to see you again."

Antonio left Lucrecia's residence free of all his doubts. He packed his things in a wicker trunk, crossed the room with padded walls where he had once swept up Leona Coralina's hair, and abandoned the Majestic that very evening, without turning back. He left behind the fabulous curves of the daughters of Ambrosius Ehinger, the peals of laughter in the middle of the night that woke the neighborhood, the fragrance of piracy mixed with the heady scent of powdered breasts, and precisely because that kingdom of passion and misfortune was part of his formative years, he was certain that he would never go back there again.

He therefore was not present when fire engulfed the Majestic a few years later, one Tuesday in July, the day a customer threw a cigarette into a puddle of gasoline, and there was nothing left of the ancient glory of the most beautiful whores in the Caribbean except ruined timbers and shreds of scorched sheets. Nor did he see that this house was so notable, so respected, and had taken such an important place in the city's collective memory that the entire population set about reconstructing it. He never knew that the council decided on a new location, that the fort of San Carlos donated timber for the rafters, that the inhabitants of El Moján gathered the barrels of coconut oil for the lamps, and that the San Juan de Dios hospital donated thirty-four iron bedsteads with their springs coated in sweet almond oil out of respect for the neighbors. He did not attend the inauguration of the New Majestic with its ramshackle fanfare of bugles and strings, under the protection of Nuestra Señora de las Nieves and a mass celebrated by the illustrious prelate Monsignor Aquiles Penazca, for by that time Antonio had already packed his bags and left for the address written on the letter to that Don Victor Emiro, where a new fate awaited him.

Don Victor Emiro Montero *de todos los santos* was a lawyer. He lived with his wife, Prudencia Rosario, née Romero, and his eight children in the El Empedrao district, next to the Santa Lucía church, in a large building whose construction he had directed in stages with each new birth. When his sons José Domingo, Manuel, and Ciro Alberto were born, he had erected a wing with two bedrooms decorated with toucans painted on the walls, then had been forced to expand that building three years later, adding two even larger rooms, since the arrival of Luis, Guillermo, and Aura had made the house too crowded.

When the twins Angela Rosa and Ana Alicia came into the world, he had the wall of the living room torn down to create two other bedrooms, with windows looking out over a garden planted with crape myrtles, and had the tub in the bathroom lengthened by a yard. Prudencia Rosario, exhausted by seven pregnancies and five miscarriages, serial caesareans, and twenty years of breastfeeding, lost thirty pounds, and her head was crowned with white hair. She was so emaciated and fragile that nobody could quite understand, whenever they saw her coming out of her house followed by her eight children, how such a host of robust cherubs could have sprung forth from the belly of this frail little woman, whom they greeted in the street with more compassion than respect.

Her two unmarried sisters, Albertina and Elena, moved in with her to lend a hand, and a nurse and a cook were also hired. Realizing that his house was being populated at an alarming rate, Don Victor Emiro had four masons come to enlarge the living room, so there was at least one room where everyone could gather. He filled it with mobiles made of bamboo and the Montero household thus became a noisy aviary where silence seemed to be banned. In the center was a long table carved from black ebony that could seat eighteen people, which was permanently set and never seen empty. When Antonio arrived at the Montero household at the end of April, into a crowd of exhausted builders and babies in linen diapers, in a home filled with builders' tools and wooden toys, his presence was scarcely noticed. Don Victor Emiro Montero, whose days flew past in a flurry of professional activities as a lawyer, of family obligations, and in the never-ending renovations of the house, was the last one to notice him.

"Who are you?" he asked one evening when he discovered him sitting in a corner of the kitchen, next to the stove, the letter in his hand.

Antonio replied serenely, "That's for you to tell me."

Don Victor Emiro Montero tore open the envelope and read the letter from Elías under his breath, standing up. He was a short man with wiry muscles, very pale skin, round glasses, and a balding head. He thought fast and always stood up straight. When he finished reading, he raised his eyes and examined Antonio with a penetrating gaze.

"What's your name?"

"Antonio."

"Did you go to school?"

"Never."

After eight children, Don Victor Emiro knew enough about school scheduling to realize in a second that the current year's enrollment period was already closed.

"You'll have to wait until the start of the next school year, young man."

Antonio lowered his eyes in disappointment. But the vitality and generosity of Don Victor, which matched the colossal size of the house he had built one birth after another, inspired him with a solution even before Antonio had time to get discouraged.

"Do you know how to read?"

"A little."

"Well then we'll find something to keep you busy," he replied.

Don Victor Emiro was a man of integrity whom no one had been able to corrupt. He had become a lawyer not only to defend justice and ensure the law was respected, but also to break the old family system that had expected all the Monteros to become sailors and spend their lives aboard ships, crossing Lake Maracaibo from one end to the other until they died at sea, in the bottom of a cabin, far away from a port. Although he had no particular calling for the law, he threw himself into that career with all the determination of an escapee, turning his back on generations of buccaneers before him, for he considered mariners to be beings with no home or parliament, who knew nothing of the laws of the land, and whose sole trace in history was a wake in the water.

His brother Elías, however, had followed that family heritage without hesitation. Despite their incontestable differences, and even if their pathways had diverged in their adolescence, they had preserved a close, irreducible brotherly connection, the anchor of which did not weaken with time and seemed even to grow stronger as they aged. A man of his word, just, with immutable principles and a serene, level-headed temperament, Don Victor Emiro had never lost touch with his tempestuous and crazy brother, even during the darkest periods when he had been lost for months in the most perilous backwaters and the many times he was presumed dead in Indigenous burial grounds. Don Victor Emiro judged his family as he judged the law.

"Despite his flaws, you have to hold on to him," he would say to his wife.

One day, his practice closed and he was forced to find new employment. Elías put him in touch with someone called Mister Barton, an obscenely wealthy man from the United States who had just bought oil concessions on the lake. When he found out that Don Victor Emiro was Elías's brother, Mister Barton hired him on the spot, found him an office, contracts, and files, and Don Victor

Emiro Montero became one of the most influential lawyers in his firm, the Caribbean Petroleum Company, in the center of Los Haticos. The business prospered on the market and made his fortune. That was why, each time he needed to pay for the addition of a new room to his enormous home, he secretly thanked Elías for having become a sailor and saving the family honor.

And so, that evening when Antonio appeared to him in the kitchen with a letter from his brother in his hand, Don Victor Emiro remembered the debt he owed Elías. And never did it even cross the old lawyer's mind, the moment their eyes met in the kitchen, that this adolescent with his sad wild expression, this boy fed with patience and fire, would one day become one of his best clients.

In the Montero household, Antonio discovered another world, that of a real family. Having never had one himself, he felt a mixture of fascination and strangeness for these eight healthy children who came home from school every evening yelling and pushing like a battalion of Cossacks, famished and filthy, while Prudencia Rosario, pregnant again, prepared industrial quantities of cornmeal arepas and large jugs of sugarcane juice with lemon, and carried huge cauldrons of soup, which her children emptied in a few minutes. The house was filled with such chaos that it was hard to say exactly how many mouths there were to feed, and the carnival atmosphere that reigned in the living room every day gave rise in

Antonio's heart to the humble desire to build a family of his own one day. This hullabaloo, this magnificent and exhausting ruckus only faded when the littlest ones went to bed and the bigger ones hung their hammocks, but also when Don Victor came home, in the twilight of the full moon, at the time when the geckos slapped their rough tongues into the cracks in the walls.

It was on one of these evenings that he appeared in Antonio's room, with his little round glasses, his pate shining in the darkness, and announced to him with a smile: "Tomorrow you'll come with me."

This was at the end of October. Don Victor found him a job as an office boy, with a salary of eight bolívares per day. Antonio devoted himself to this new occupation with the same determination with which he had once honored his contract at the Majestic, and with the same strength he had deployed to build Samuel Smith's wall to stop the oil reaching the lake. Four times a day, he was brought with other workers from the lake's marketplace on the docks to the offices in La Rosa, on a motor barge loaded with barrels and crates of rum, with men who played dominoes and shot sleeping iguanas for target practice.

He was energetic and made his mark, such that he climbed the pyramid of employees to become an apprentice in mechanography with the director, Mister Barton. Everything happened with such fluidity, such energy, that the year came to an end without him noticing.

Antonio completely forgot about school registrations, and was convinced that he had at last found his path in the annunciatory cogwheels of mechanography.

Contrary to Don Victor Emiro, he presented no signs of eagerness in fulfilling the request of Captain Elías's letter. He continued to progress up the stagnant and complex hierarchy of employees as indifferently as he perforated the eighty-column cards. He learned the invoicing and stock-management systems, and got used to the crashing noise of the large data-processing machines, letting himself be guided by his patient instinct, and resolved to one day become a secretary.

But his plans were abruptly overthrown during the first rains of September. One morning, two days before the beginning of the school year, during a meeting with the company's entire management team, Don Victor Emiro entered Mister Barton's office and, with no warning or other announcement, came to put Antonio's letter of resignation on his desk. Mister Barton, surprised by this unexpected decision, accepted it with regret.

"Antonio has made a lot of progress since his arrival. I had thought to make him my personal mechanographer. He could earn a very decent salary."

Don Victor Emiro Montero did not hesitate. He then expressed what Antonio himself was unaware of as his true vocation in life.

"I beg your pardon, Mister Barton, but Antonio will be neither a scribe nor a secretary." He added with premonitory conviction: "Antonio will be a doctor."

This certainty, of which Antonio understood the portent only fifteen years later, was the sole true proof of love that Don Victor ever gave him. For his part, Don Victor could never have imagined, the day he received his brother's letter while leaning on the sink in the kitchen, seeing that famished boy with no future sitting before him, that he would choose such an arduous career as medicine for him, and load onto Antonio's shoulders a burden that he himself would not have been able to bear. He suspected, seeing Antonio at work, observing his abnegation and strength, that he was more than ready to take up a noble challenge, one endowed with the grandeur that perhaps only children dropped on church steps could appreciate.

Don Victor Emiro thus stood by his word. He enrolled Antonio in the Hermágoras Chávez school. When he gave his date of birth, the headmistress let out a slight cry of surprise at discovering that Antonio was fifteen years old on his first day of school. Don Victor, dressed in his black suit, his collar tightened by a bow tie, and his little round glasses set severely on his nose, had just given him a banknote taken from the bundle that Elías had included in the letter, to cover the week's expenses.

"As long as you are studying, you won't have to work."

Although he was much older than the others, Antonio looked like a little child with his slate chalkboard in his hand, his colored pencils, and his cloth pencil case on which Prudencia Rosario had embroidered his initials. To begin with, the first signs of an inner change were barely perceptible. He earned good grades, learned algebra, and developed such an interest in his studies that he thought of mechanography as nothing more than an error in his past. His schooling allowed the seed of his taste for knowledge, his thirst for understanding, to grow. His schoolboy life made him gain weight, for his physical activity had decreased. It deepened the furrows on his brow and channeled his strength. He remained as he always had been, tenacious and obstinate, with something about him that was feline, ready to pounce, but through hard work he also gained a kind of solitary concentration that made him calmer. His hours spent catching up with the others, rewriting his homework hundreds of times, improving the quality of his penmanship, all that silent work he completed in the midst of the infernal racket of the Montero family, secluded in a room at the back of the house, endowed him with a severe expression. He allowed himself to believe in this new dream, first vicariously, then out of his own conviction, and developed the confident bearing of those who are committed to a goal.

He completed his secondary education at the federal boys' school, not far from the convent on Plaza Baralt, under the direction of Doctor Jesús Enriquez Lossada. The school's motto was *post nubila phoebus*—after the clouds, the sun—engraved in stone at the front door, and those strange erudite sounds, so unlike the tropical lightness of his own language, remained tattooed in his memory like an oracle.

He was such a good student and made up for his late start so well that he was given a free ticket every week to El Metro movie house. This was an agreement reached between the manager of the cinema and the teacher Señor Córdoba to stimulate young people in their studies. The ticket could only be won thanks to a competition between all the girls and boys who were the best students in the district. Every Wednesday, in Señor Córdoba's classroom, this competition plunged the highest-performing students into pitched battles in spelling and mathematics, of which the only real effect was to give Antonio, besides an exhaustive knowledge of the films of the 1930s, the opportunity to meet the girl who would become the love of his life, Ana María Rodríguez.

The first time he saw her, Ana María presented herself for the exam at three o'clock on the dot, with her pencil case under her arm and an air of concentration. Dressed in a long black pleated dress with a white bow at the back, she was a slender girl and very discreet. To begin with, Antonio thought her quite ordinary, rather vapid in fact, and completely devoid of the impetuous charms of the women with outrageous laughs and voluptuous curves who had peopled his imagination since the explosive time of the Majestic. Her father, a certain Chinco Rodríguez, a typographer from Táchira who was well-known throughout the neighborhood for his socialist ideas, came to drop her off and collect her every day.

One Wednesday after the next, she won. From the day she started participating in the competitions, she claimed all the cinema tickets. Antonio, who had become used to reigning over this prize, redoubled his efforts to beat her. Every afternoon that they faced off against each other, the tension that invaded Señor Córdoba's classroom was so palpable you could have touched it. Tired of losing all the time, at the tenth competition one Wednesday in March, Antonio arrived with a warrior's resolution, so much so that the other students withdrew and only Ana María and he remained facing each other, as in a battle of Cyclopes in an irreducible arena, leading everyone to understand that a silent jousting match between them had begun. Antonio remained standing during the entire exam. When he was finished, he waited for the results in the same position, his gaze fixed on the examiners. That time, he was the one to prevail. He was given the cinema ticket. He took it with a solemn expression and turned to Ana María.

"I hate going to the movies by myself."

And then, in a chivalrous gesture, he offered her the ticket he had just won. She was not so much surprised by the invitation as by the entitled tone in which it was uttered. In a voice that brooked no response, she respectfully rejected the ticket.

"You have just demonstrated your intelligence," she said. "Don't ruin everything by saying something stupid."

This statement, which Antonio ruminated over for a long time, seemed to him to be a triumph of freedom and audacity. He could never quite understand what attracted him to her. The threat she represented, the murmur of a new world, the sovereignty of her gaze, there was something impregnable and sacred in this girl that made him shudder. Antonio could no longer go for a walk without thinking about her with a mixture of desire and defiance. That feeling seemed so heavy, and the memory of Ana María was so stubborn and insistent, that after ten days, he confided it to a friend.

"She's too short," he said.

"That's true," Antonio replied. "She always is the shortest in the room. But everyone has to raise their eyes to speak to her."

Ana María tormented him unceasingly. He felt for her the same feverish emotion that had deprived him of sleep all those years ago, after his first morning of lovemaking with Leona Coralina at the Majestic, but this time with a deeper, more intense dimension, to which were added ships that capsized but never sank. He tried to run into her again by wandering through the corridors of the school of Missia Alcina, agitated by her image, keeping watch for her at each table in the library, on each stone staircase, but he had to resign himself to seeing her only in the heady visions that haunted his dreams.

He found out her address. A week later, exhausted from thinking about her so much, he decided to wait for her near her house. One Wednesday, with a fluttering heart and shaking hands, he presented himself at her front door, and when he saw her come out, wearing a low-cut dress with a white collar and raffia boots, he was certain that she was the woman he should love. She passed in front of him and he could not help asking her, "What do I have to do to marry you?"

But Ana María, showing no surprise, looked at him coldly.

"How easy it must be to be a man," she said. "To be able to walk down the street and say what you want."

Antonio did not know what to reply. Faced with his silence, she added, "You should know that I will be a doctor before I become a wife, señor."

"You too?"

She was silent for a moment, then looked at him from head to toe.

"You wouldn't be up to it anyway."

"Why not?" Antonio asked, his pride stung.

Ana María remained serious and declared, in a voice full of scorn and all the irony of the world, "Because I will only marry the man who can tell me the most beautiful love story."

Antonio knew nothing about love. He had grown up in a brothel where love stories were only ruses to get a discount on the price of favors. He had known only women who would twirl their corsets and petticoats over their heads for a few pesos, girls who flaunted their satanic powers in the darkness and whose faithfulness and obedience cost a surcharge. All he knew about women were the acrobatics of intimacy and the cunning of experience, the prudence when faced with new customers and the little treats given to regulars, but none of them had ever told him a love story. The only ones he knew were those that had germinated in the fantasies of the craziest lieutenants, of the most perverse sailors, of the most corrupt priests, the most concupiscent politicians, and never had he imagined that anyone would offer a flower to someone else without expecting a petal in return.

Incapable of finding a single story worth telling in all his memories, a single poem worthy of his sentiments, a single romantic line from his misspent youth in cabarets, he threw in the towel and renounced Ana María, resigning himself to finishing his life as a bachelor. It was his friend Paz Galarraga who, when he heard about the whole affair, sat him down at a table at Café Maurice and said, looking him straight in the eyes, "No one ever makes anything up, Antonio. The greatest love stories are ten a penny."

Those words, the ardent desire to engage in this battle, and the tenacity that he had always shown, then inspired him with an idea. The next day, at dawn, he cut out a piece of cardboard, took two stools, and headed with a decisive step to the bus station, which was the most crowded place in the area, a veritable anthill. In the middle of the central concourse, he set up his stools facing each other. He put down the cardboard sign, on which he had painted these words in black so they would be visible from a distance: I LISTEN TO LOVE STORIES.

After half an hour, a man with a round belly introduced himself as Nicanor Melaza. He had a bald head and wore gold-rimmed glasses beneath his glowing forehead, and carried a suitcase under his arm. Although he was perspiring in the unbearable heat of the bus station, he did not take off a scarf made of Belgian silk, which he had knotted around his neck and held with a topaz pin. The crowd bustling around him made him nervous. But when he sat down on the little stool facing Antonio and started telling his story, the return of those happy memories made him feel calm.

While dabbing his forehead with his handkerchief, he launched into the story of a legend that took place on the other side of the country, in a village called La Tuerta, the one-eyed lady, about a woman who was struck with blindness one day and whose husband, out of love, had poked out his own eyes to share her darkness. One morning, as suddenly as she had lost her sight, she regained it, and when she learned of her husband's folly, she pierced only one of her eyes, so that she could keep the other to guide him until his death.

Antonio, who knew the virtue of silence from Mute Teresa, did not interrupt Nicanor Melaza's account. He started copying down his words, hunched over the pages of his notebook with such reverence and concentration that he did not notice the group of passengers that had formed around him. It was Nicanor Melaza who stopped in the middle of a phrase to remark, "You appear to have some success."

Antonio raised his eyes and saw the line. There were men and women waiting their turn, standing one behind the other, while they had a stopover or some time before their bus departed, holding baskets of provisions on their shoulders, dragging trunks with canoe ropes, or carrying sacks full of crockery and old inheritances. In the hubbub of the bus station, their stomachs emptied by the trials of their journeys, they came forward one after the next throughout the whole morning with the solemnity of a religious procession. This is how he learned the story of Roberta Manzanares, who had boarded an iron ship to flee poverty in Argentina and join her brother in Portugal, but she had fallen in love with the ship's captain and never disembarked in Lisbon, but stayed on board and continued the voyage by his side for fifty years, until his last shipwreck.

A Turkish man from Anatolia, who was quite wealthy, refused to leave his son's tomb after his funeral and, when evening came and he could not find sleep, tried to exhume him so he could lie down by his side. Claudia Miraflores, a lady dressed all in white and with flowers in her hair, told him the story of her mother, a woman whose delicate skin was allergic to sunlight and whose husband had built a house with no windows and only one door, which was opened only at night, such that they lived and died without knowing about the decrepitude of their aging bodies, each imagining the other as they were when they first met, each lighting the darkness for the other.

To begin with, Antonio did not see this as anything more than a game. As devoted as a copyist monk to the loyalty of his storytellers' confidences, he made them spell out all the names, repeat the dates, clarify any imprecisions. Even though he found these stories touching, he did not let himself be carried away by their tellers' feverish sensitivity or their immodest tears but just listened politely. He studied the anatomy of love as one studies a body under dissection. But little by little he was overtaken by a curiosity that went beyond the challenge he had set himself, as if his head had been filled with a torrent of red roses. Some people talked about how their ancestors had first fallen in love a hundred and fifty years ago, telling their story with such fervor that it sounded like breaking news. Others related what they had read in a novel or overheard at a café, anecdotes they had gleaned here or there and disguised or embellished like dolls, and these accounts all led him to wonder whether there was a single story in the world that was not about love.

Travelers would arrive from everywhere, in couples and singly, truck drivers and passengers, who suddenly transported him into a parallel universe made of stolen kisses and kept promises. He learned the story of Astrid Medina who, during the war in the Pacific, had received a love letter from a soldier that was addressed to another woman and decided to answer it, starting an epistolary relationship of twenty years with a man she never met.

The one about a pistolero with curly hair who was in love with a Peruvian woman from Colca, Lea Simonetta, who spent his entire life writing a fable about a country where they could be free to love. The one about a Dominican beauty named Dulce Concepción, who set out for Canaima in order to revive an old love she had for a lady violinist whom she had shot twice with a revolver. And a thousand and one other stories that were overwhelming in their beauty and so convoluted and implausible that Antonio wished he could build a library right there in the middle of the bus station in order to preserve them all.

One evening, when a Jewish woman was telling him how she met her husband during a Sephardic diaspora, she asked Antonio, "So what are you going to do with all these stories, then?"

Antonio realized that his notebook was almost filled, although there were still a few empty pages left. It was bursting with courageous embraces and rediscovered illusions, with commitment and virtuosity, and with hundreds of unknown names that seemed to him to belong to a single man. He shut the notebook and replied, "I'm going off to live my own story."

Many years later, as a respected and respectable man, during the afternoon when he was inaugurating the new street that would bear his name, Antonio was easily able to return to the memory of the morning when, with his full notebook, he searched for Ana María in all the corners of her school. He found her sitting under a mango tree. That morning the light shone with the purest clarity, free from any dust or ash. Antonio looked at her as he had imagined her in the narration of his dreams, as if she had just finished being created, with that same limpidity, with a resemblance to his visions that was so astonishing that he believed that this scene was occurring for the second time. He only came to when Ana María, seeing him standing there with his arms akimbo, looked up at him. That is when Antonio said in a decisive voice, "I do not know which is the most beautiful love story. But here are a thousand of them."

He set the notebook from the central bus station on her knees. Then he added, "I propose we write our own."

Ana María

The fabulous destiny of *doctora* Ana María Rodríguez began one February 14th, off the coast of Sinamaica, the day a fisherman named Martín Gámez made a discovery that was one of the strangest Maracaibo had known. It had been raining all month, and the high tides of the last few days had transformed the beach of Caimare Chico into a heap of muddy seaweed and fish carcasses. The shore was covered so completely that when Martín Gámez came in from fishing at dawn, at around five o'clock, it was almost impossible to distinguish the animals from the piles of kelp.

When he cautiously approached, he first thought that it was a gray octopus, lying there like a shipwreck, which must have gotten tangled in the ribbons of seaweed and not been able to get back to the water. Then he noticed that it had neither tentacles nor suction cups, only two large side wings and a silver belly, and decided it was an upturned tortoise. But it was only when he touched it with a stick and the animal straightened up suddenly on its two owl-like legs that Martín Gámez understood that he had just discovered a penguin in the middle of the Caribbean.

Terrorized by this creature that seemed to portend the apocalypse, he went off to alert Alejandro Crespo, a Costa Rican who had a beach kiosk a few yards away.

They came back at a run and examined the penguin, making the sign of the cross on their foreheads with a mixture of fear and revulsion, murmuring a discreet "*Virgen María*" without being brave enough to touch it. It had intense red eyes, like two blazing poppies, a gray-black coat of an undefinable color, and on its back was a tuft of soft feathers as smooth and supple as the cloth of a bowler hat. Although it was close to 105°F, it seemed to be tolerating the heat with dignity. It contemplated them loftily from its twenty inch height with almost Roman bravura. The crossing had made it lose some of the feathers from its head, and a piece of its wing had been bitten off by a sea leopard along with a few claws from its feet, but it had preserved its natural elegance, highlighted by two dainty yellow crests shaped like eyebrows, which made the fishermen think it was perhaps a female, as they were the only ones that could survive such an odyssey.

Alejandro Crespo took a few minutes to get over his perplexity.

"Call the village," he told Martín Gámez. "We need to find out if there are more of them."

With the help of a dozen men, a search was organized on the beach. Armed with shovels and rakes to turn over the piles of seaweed, they spent all morning shaking down the sea grape trees along the coast, set the dogs into the bushes, tracked the slightest movement in the palm trees, and since they found nothing, they concluded that there was probably only a single individual of the species in the world. The penguin was put into a sack of serge canvas to protect it from the sun and transported to the kiosk. The man carrying it felt as if it were heavier than a whale, but he assumed that was because of the burden of exile. The penguin was settled into the only refrigerator on the beach, on top of a crate of beer bottles between two blocks of ice, and when it felt that cold surface, no doubt for the first time in months, it threw itself at the frozen panel and remained motionless with its belly stuck to it, its beak tucked into its chest and eyes closed, as if it were asleep.

Within a few hours, all of Maracaibo had heard the news that a penguin had washed up on its shores. The rumor reached the institute of natural sciences whose director, Augustín Pérez Piñango, a man with harmonious features and as tall as a votive candle, was filled with alarm. He had been at the head of the institute for the last four years and had sought to enrich his knowledge of rare species with encyclopedic zeal. He had once been called regarding a narwhal tusk that was found in the mud of a farmyard, for a manatee that had got lost in the swamps of Perijá, and for a whale that swam up the Río Escalante all the way to Santa Bárbara. He would never have imagined that he would ever be told about the extravagant capture of a penguin that swam up from the pole to these tropical waters and survived six thousand miles of dangers. He jumped into a car and drove along the northern road toward Sinamaica.

When he arrived at the beach of Caimare Chico, he found the entire village crowded around the kiosk.

Alejandro Crespo, as proud as a bishop, was making people pay a bolívar to raise the lid on his refrigerator to show the penguin. In a ruckus of laughter, everyone had an opinion about the animal's fate. Some said that it should be thrown back to sea where its instinct would allow it to return to polar waters. Others suggested an auction be organized right there on the spot, at the kiosk, before the authorities arrived. Still others said that it should be let out, put up high somewhere, and pushed to see if it could fly. But Augustín Pérez Piñango, who was a self-taught naturalist, an intelligent and sensitive man who had also studied musicology and linguistics, planted himself valiantly in front of Alejandro Crespo and demanded that the refrigerator be opened for him.

"That'll be one bolívar if you want to see the wild beast," Crespo said.

"The only wild beast in this room is you, señor. In the name of science, open up," he said with authority.

To give additional weight to his words, he held up his card from the institute so that everyone could see it, and the lid was duly raised. In the darkness inside, he could just see a slumped black mass and, in the middle of it, a vermillion glow that might be an iris. The penguin was standing huddled into a corner, its back hunched, its body sunk over its feet. It was face on, but had turned its head to the side. It fixed the man with its single fiery eye, red and menacing, and Pérez Piñango found it sublime. The penguin seemed to him to be a legendary creature, unreal and even further mythicized by its migration and exodus, and in its eye there appeared to be a form of subtle judgment, an animal intelligence that unsettled the naturalist.

"That's not a wild beast," he said with emotion. "That is a southern rockhopper, a *Eudyptes chrysocome*."

That name, despite its erudite sound, was not convincing to the assembled crowd. A lady carrying shopping bags came forward.

"Well, I think his name is Policarpio."

The crowd acquiesced in a collective murmur. A bucket of fish was brought to the penguin, which he devoured with a voracious appetite. While he was eating, a refrigerated truck arrived to take him to Maracaibo, and it took four men to carry the animal to its back doors, for not only was he heavier than before but he was struggling ferociously, pecking away at them and making animal cries that no one had ever heard before.

After an hour driving along the zigzags of the arid plains, when the doors of the truck were opened, he was found lying on his side, still alive, bathing in a puddle of vomit from which an odor of rotted seaweed and mashed fish was emanating.

"It's a species that easily gets land sick," said Augustín Pérez Piñango apologetically.

The following day, a veterinarian came to take his pulse, but realized he had no clue how to measure it, for this was the first time he had ever touched a penguin. After a week, American and German specialists arrived, who had come all the way from their research centers in order to photograph him, study his behavior, habits, nutritional needs, and endurance capacity in order to understand how this animal could adjust with such tenacity to a tropical climate.

Every single newspaper carried an article about Policarpio, now the town's mascot, who for some journalists had become the last of its species and for others the first of an invasion yet to come. An announcement was published to find out whether a foreign vessel or a marine zoo had noticed a missing animal. Since nobody came forward, the thought was that he had perhaps escaped from a trawler engaged in the illegal traffic in rare species. This hypothesis remained the most plausible one. After a few weeks his gestures were recorded and classified with such exhaustive detail, his sleeping patterns were archived with such solicitude, that more was learned about this polar bird than about the pink flamingos that had lived on the lakeside for the last two thousand years.

He was sent to the zoo in Maracaibo where he was exhibited for six months. It cost four lochas to see him, and even so, around three hundred thousand people apparently came to visit him. But Policarpio, in the large cage in which he had been placed, turned his back on the crowds. All anyone could see was the back of his head, his lowered neck, his shoulders, and the little tail sticking out of the bottom of his coat like a clenched fist. He stood motionless for hours, his eyes closed, his beak tucked into his chest, his shoulders hunched, trying to withstand the heat of the tropics with an economy of movement. He had an air of immense sadness. Anyone would think he was a statue carved out of ebony and set down in a corner.

On August 28th, because the penguin was not moving, a child threw a stone at him to try to make him react. Policarpio was hit on the side of the head and swayed a little. He reached up his wing to protect his face. All his muscles had tensed from the shock of the blow. Two drops of blood stained the immaculate whiteness of his belly. Later on the press would say that the penguin had turned around for the first time, thrown a last majestic glance at the crowd, its beak dripping with blood, without a cry or complaint but with the superiority of noble races, and that the red flames of his eyes had illuminated the entire zoo for an instant. He fell headfirst into a small pond.

That August 28th, at three minutes past 9:00 a.m., he died of a cerebral hemorrhage, and more than a few people would say that it was ironic for a penguin to swim six thousand miles of the ocean only to drown in a puddle.

Hundreds of people filed by to see Policarpio's embalmed body at the institute, in a little mausoleum built for him by Doctor Pons. The novelist Salvador Garmendia wrote a book about him. His name was given to two grocery stores, to the Polo ice-cream brand, to a frozen-foods company, and a band of *gaiteros* composed a song in his memory that was so famous during the local festivals that the crossroads of El Tránsito and El Saladillo would become known to this day as El Pingüino district. But before the day came when *doctora* Ana María Rodríguez would inherit a gold penguin, before the instant when the story of that animal would start following the family history for several generations, first there was a jeweler who also reached the coast of Zulia.

One week after Policarpio's death, a man arrived in Maracaibo on a foreign vessel one morning. He had a wide forehead and black hair. A jeweler of some thirty years, with lacustrine green eyes, hooded eyelids, and tight lips, he entered the main street with strange instruments under his arm that no one had ever seen before. He brought with him new jewelry techniques, took Venezuelan citizenship, married, had one son, and founded a small jewelry store on Calle Victorino Meadeb. The tragic history of Policarpio of Maracaibo inspired him to design a brooch, a magnificent jewel in the shape of a penguin, carved in profile with feathers of gold leaf, feet of encrusted emeralds, a beak of lapis lazuli, and a ruby eye. Although this objet d'art would have been worth a fortune, he decided not to put it up for sale but to give it to his only child, that son, as a present at his birth, and that was how José de la Chiquinquirá, whom everyone affectionately called Chinco, happened to acquire that inheritance of gemstones, which he kept for years in a wooden case.

Chinco did not take his father's place in the back room of the jewelry store. When he turned twenty, he refused to replace him in the business and became a typographer for a French company that was building a railway in the province of Táchira. He started the first machinist union, was active in civic struggles and claims, was in charge of setting the agenda for workers' meetings, and was convinced that the only jewels that should adorn a man's chest were those of liberty and social justice. His father secretly regretted his son's decision, realizing that he understood nothing of the jewelry business but everything about class struggle, that he lived surrounded not by fine stones but by factory workers, and that he was more moved by the injustices in the metallurgy industry than by the value of precious metals. One Sunday, as Chinco was writing a speech for the union, his father asked him, "Do you intend to marry a woman or the revolution?"

Chinco, who was a cheerful, energetic young man, endowed with fine dreamy eyes, had a discreet smile that let nothing slip. "Maybe a threesome?" he said without thinking. His father knew him, however, and was aware that a name was already occupying his son's dreams, having found him one day at sunset on the main square, waiting for a young woman to pass by. He was obviously concentrating not on organizing union meetings but on imagining secret rendezvous, stolen kisses, and a passion consummated between two doorsteps.

And thus, at a time when the roots of a revolt were starting to grow, when the first socialist ideas were beginning to germinate, when the value of an old aristocratic gold brooch had no place anymore, the penguin never saw the light of day until Chinco decided to marry a certain Eva Rosa.

Eva Rosa was the daughter of an embroiderer on the Calle San José, a clairvoyant in fragile health, who was said to be able to read the future in the patterns of fabric, but who was unable to predict from the blood in her own handkerchiefs an aggressive case of pneumonia that carried her off at thirty. Eva Rosa's widower father, Papa Zoilo Rodríguez, was a collector of guns and a severe and uncompromising man with a tall wiry body, whose tone of voice was reminiscent of the authority of the first military chiefs of the independence. Despite her mother's skeletal figure and her father's rectilinear one, where there was no excess of flesh, no abundance or profusion, Eva Rosa was all opulence, overflow, prodigality. She looked like one of those women with sensuous and lively eyes, full hips and exuberant breasts, whose round belly could accommodate a thousand children. Her skin was so pale and of such translucent whiteness that it seemed to have been kneaded out of goat milk.

However, her abundant flesh was constrained by the weight of that family name, Rodríguez, by the rigidity of her austere father who had raised her alone in the servitude of the Catholic Church, and by an incredible number of layers of skirts, corsets, and closed collars, which she was allowed to remove only when she was going to sleep. The covetable realm of her body, that explosive femininity that would have made any princess blush, was sequestered away from the world behind ramparts of metal clasps, knots, and ribbons, and by the incorruptible vigilance of her father, who was ferociously jealous at even the idea that a man might dare to breathe the same air as she did. He forbade her from going out alone during the day, and in the evenings, when the fading light made women's beauty deceptive, he would take her for a stroll around the square, his face closed and his mood churlish, holding her by the arm.

The young men sitting on the wall of the jetty would watch this mythological creature pass by with her eyes full of sorrow, and although she always maintained an affable expression and a serene smile, none of them ever dared say a word to her, not out of fear of Papa Zoilo's collection of guns but out of reluctance to break the innocent magic of this mirage.

Papa Zoilo had just acquired a sixteenth-century weapon, an arquebus used by Captain Pedro Vicente Maldonado during the period of the foundation of Nueva Zamora de Maracaibo, an iron jewel of a gun engraved with Latin mottoes and acanthus leaves, when Eva Rosa got her first period. Troubled by this unexpected apparition of nature, he made her a member of the society of young ladies adored by the *Purísima Virgen María*. From seven in the morning onward, she could be seen crossing the street with a bevy of girls dressed in white with flowers in their hair, all scented flesh and stifled giggles, clasping a mango-wood cross in her fist and sheltering the perfection of her skin behind a Spanish fan.

On the Calle San José, it was the custom in the evenings that, after having prayed the rosary to all the saints of the church, young ladies would linger at their windows at dusk, protected by the iron railings, to watch the world go by under their balconies. No one could imagine what the beautiful Eva Rosa was looking for as she observed the comings and goings in the street from her window shutters during all those hours, during all those evenings, gazing at the same people on the same sidewalk, with her voluptuous and volcanic body strangled by the impenetrable ways of the Lord, and she would have grown old behind those shutters, in the stifling shadow of her father, if she had not one evening discovered a sealed envelope wedged between the arabesques of the railing. Inside she found the gold brooch shaped like a penguin. A note accompanied this jewel: "I will wait for you tomorrow evening behind the church."

It was signed "*El pingüino.*" Eva Rosa, who had been reared by five centuries of repression and subjugation to refuse all advances, who had been walled up behind the arrow slits and gun loops of sixteen years of catechism, who had been dried out like a moat by a continent of fortresses and silences, was so struck by this audacity that she was immediately fascinated. Her splendid paradise of golden rays and immaculate cherubs vanished, and the promise of a sin so profound, of an error so grave, made her vault, in one night, over the chasm that since childhood had separated her from her most secret desires.

During the entire following day, she thought about this rendezvous with impatience. When the time arrived and she found the right excuse to escape from the watchful eyes of Papa Zoilo, she walked hastily to the back of the church, her heart pounding in her chest, her mouth dry, and her stomach full of crazed bees. She found a young man standing there, leaning against a silver pine tree, drawing stars on the ground with the tip of his shoe. Chinco raised his eyes to hers. He smiled at her. Eva Rosa, paralyzed, found him so charming, so handsome, that she turned on her heels and left at once.

Chinco remained alone, without having had the time to look at her properly, but that second when she had been a fleeting apparition was enough for him to imagine her in his most passionate dreams. The image of this young lady of God left him no rest. He spent his nights in delirium, imagining all kinds of bacchanalia under his sheets. He battled lusty demons, astonished at the mesmerizing youth of the creature he had called forth under his blanket, and who could never suspect that on the other side of the Calle San José lived the best lover she would ever have.

One morning, Chinco crossed the street with determination and, before knocking at the door of the Rodríguez family home, made the sign of the cross three times. It was Papa Zoilo who opened the door, with his arquebus slung over his shoulder, which he had been greasing with a dirty rag.

"Don Zoilo Rodríguez," Chinco said in a firm but humble tone, "I have come to ask for your daughter's hand."

Papa Zoilo, standing there like a jailer on the doorstep, stared at him in silence. Chinco could read no expression on his face.

"You must have the wrong door," he replied. "My daughter is already married to God."

Eva Rosa, who had followed this whole scene from her window, hiding behind her shutters, felt humiliated. She was so sickened to have been handed into slavery to the angels and so vexed by these words, that from that day forward, as if revealed unto herself, she no longer wished to offer her youth to a man she had never seen and could never touch. Something inside her had awoken. It was no longer in heaven that she searched for an answer but in the vigorous pulsation of her own heart. The following day, she wrote the same message on a piece of paper: "I will wait for you tomorrow evening behind the church."

She signed it "*La pingüina*" and stuck the paper to the balustrade, at the very spot where she had found the envelope with the brooch a few days previously. She waited for evening with the resolution of offering this man what she would henceforth deny to God. Eva Rosa saw Chinco a second time against the tree behind the church, then a third, and it would not take many clandestine encounters to unlatch all the padlocks that religion had fastened around her modesty and to disrobe her of all the drapery of virtue against the silvery bark of that old pine.

She gave herself to him with such ignorance of the ways of love that she forgot to count her days. Such that when she was late with her cycle, she tightened her corsets with more firmness and hid her pregnancy behind a fortress of iron stays, convinced that her father would never discover the truth.

But Maracaibo was a village. It was in the café that Papa Zoilo learned the news that everyone already knew. The baker Yvan Zwan, the son of an Englishman from Manchester, unaware of Zoilo's presence, revealed at a table that a lucky man had finally managed to get a penguin into little Eva Rosa's belly. Zoilo was seized by such fury that he overturned all the furniture in the café and fought like an old stag, stormed out shouting profanities, smashed all the mirrors he found in his path, and when he arrived home, found his daughter serenely sitting on the veranda embroidering a shawl.

"Wait here," he said. "I'm going to kill you."

He went into his shop, took down from the wall the sixteenth-century gun that Pedro Maldonado had used long ago to hunt jaguars during the foundation of Maracaibo, and pointed it at his daughter. Eva Rosa was horrified but had the quick reaction of shutting the first door she could find to protect herself.

The bullet that had been sleeping in the barrel for four centuries crossed the street with all the legacy of churches and temples built in the middle of jungles, flew over the pavement and the stray dogs, found a way between the horses and the candy sellers, and went even farther, over the fields and grasses of Guajira, continued through the sleepless nights inhabited by giant frogs and metallic beetles, penetrated the forests crowded with soothsayers who read the future in the dances of bats, descended into the steep *cañones* where the pearl smugglers dive down to break off teardrops of coral, reached the depths of the bowels of Catatumbo, at the heart of the mermaids' nests, went past the banks of the Perijá which polished the bellies of canoes one wave after another, and flew up to the sources of the Río Magdalena, where long ago twelve hundred soldiers had marched through the dawns populated by birds whose names they did not know, opening pathways with machetes and Christian prayers, wearing heavy gold crosses underneath their armor, convinced that they were at last conquering what the alchemists of Navarra had called God's New Garden, and that bullet, which went through all of time and traveled through all the ravines of memory and the last plantations of love, returned to Maracaibo into the little Calle San José and stopped its race in the wood of the door of the Rodríguez family home, one yard away from Eva Rosa's belly where Ana María Rodríguez, who would soon be called *la doctora* by the entire country, lay asleep, waiting to be born.

Eva Rosa, who was six months pregnant and saved by this miracle, sought refuge at Chinco's house. Overcome with another fit of rage, Papa Zoilo forbade his daughter from ever setting foot in his house again and decreed that her name would never be spoken. She was taken in by her mother-in-law, the very dignified Mama Concha, in that dwelling of typographers and machinists where almost eleven old people were living. Three months later, she gave birth in a candlelit room to a perfectly healthy baby girl who was named Ana María. When Eva Rosa crossed the street in the other direction to go home for the first time since her banishment, Papa Zoilo received her with severity.

"Take a look at your granddaughter at least once," she said.

Zoilo hesitated, but his daughter's fragile dignity, her innocent light and openhearted trust made him waver for a moment in the rigidity of his decision. He took the baby into his arms, and from that day forth until the hour of his death, it was impossible for him to resist her. That very evening, he took down his arquebus, wrapped it in a kitchen tablecloth, got in a boat, and paddled out into the night of the lake until he could no longer see the city lights. Then, all alone on the water, he threw the gun overboard and watched it drown as tears rolled down his face. This was something of a resurrection for him.

The day after Ana María's birth, her ears were pierced with gold studs and her neck was strung with beads made of Mucuna grains to ward off evil. Bracelets made of shells were looped around her wrists, amulets were tucked into the sheets at each corner of her bed, essences of aloe leaves were rubbed onto her neck, rosaries hung on the bars of her cot, and a priest was brought from Coro so that she could be blessed with a discreet cross of ash on her forehead. At the end of her first week, she looked like a shaman's doll, loaded down with colored trinkets and Indigenous jewelry, and every single woman from the neighborhood passed through the Rodríguez living room to look at the child with the same curiosity and the same incredulity as that of the inhabitants of Caimare Chico when they had contemplated the penguin long ago. When Ana María was three years old, Eva Rosa took her behind the church one day, sat down against the gray pine tree with her on her lap, and put the gold penguin brooch into her hands.

"Now you are the only one who can wear it," she said softly.

Ana María grew up in Calle Nueva Venecia with the brooch forever pinned to her chest, in a house whose residents were so numerous that everyone lost count. There were three aunts, one of whom was married to a man called Rafael Barroso, and their three children, Edicta, Hilda, and little Alirio. In a room on the upper floor lived Mama Concha and her mother, an ancient lady who was almost blind and lit candles to José Gregorio Hernández, and three old people, distant cousins of Rafael Barroso, who had no other place to live, Mama Lina, Tía África, and Fransisco Antonio Alvarez, a veteran of several wars fought at the Colombian border under the command of Gómez, whom Ana María started tenderly calling Papapa. In the kitchen, the governess Carmela Ramos del Valle, an eternal spinster who still dreamed of a wonderful love story, was losing the best years of her life standing behind the countertop and miraculously feeding the whole household, and Doña Elvirita, an ageless pianist, who had been trying for twenty years to publish a collection of poems entitled *The Kingdom of the Poor.* The house on Calle Nueva Venecia was so crowded that when Mama Lina died in one of the back rooms, one stormy Tuesday, no one noticed until two days later, when a repulsive smell had spread through the rooms on the upper floor and a macaw with red plumage, perched on the window ledge, had started tapping on the pane with its black beak.

But Eva Rosa and Chinco's love story did not survive the vagaries of passion. Chinco succumbed to other temptations and Eva Rosa, whose years of catechism and moral rigor were by then no more than a distant memory, fell pregnant by the neighbor and had a second daughter. This neighbor refused to recognize his child of adultery, and in this scarcity of love she became a condemned being. That is why, one day when she was fifteen and her father asked her if she wanted to take on his family name, she replied proudly, "I already bear it without having to pronounce it."

Eva Rosa, after giving birth to two daughters from two different men, married a third, a certain Laplacelieri, the son of Italian immigrants from Tuscany who had arrived at the end of the nineteenth century to build an arsenal on the port, with whom she had two boys, Humberto and Jésus. Busy with her new family, she rarely visited Chinco, that first man she had desired so ardently against the pine tree behind the church, and it was therefore he who raised Ana María.

Although she was healthy, it took a long time for Ana María to get used to life. She remained silent, absorbed by a toy in a corner of the room, without exploring the space around her. Until she was three, nothing really attracted her attention. Chinco, who was the most involved father Maracaibo had ever known and whose daughter was his sole real treasure, could not understand where this phlegmatic nature had come from.

When she was six years old, Chinco enrolled her in the school of Nuestra Señora del Pilar, where she started learning deportment with Madre Lorenza Casado, a nun from Aragon and an intransigent woman whose strong character was the legacy of years of convents and retreats, who imposed dominical masses, daily rosaries, communion every first Friday, novenas and triduums, a whole series of obligations so precise and numerous that Ana María had no time left to dream. Chinco got used to her nebulous and uncertain personality, trusting in the courage of the Scriptures, until the evening when, on returning home from school, she held out a piece of paper with a note from Madre Lorenza Casado. When Chinco unfolded the paper, surprise flit across his face. In front of the entire family gathered together, he read it aloud: "Your daughter is a genius. She has nothing to do in this institution. Educate her at home."

No one could ever figure out whether it was the letter from the nun, giving up school, or the proximity with her father that modified Ana María's behavior, but from that evening onward, she became a different person. She started participating in the life of the household and studying with such voracity that everyone was worried, so radical was the transformation. She was so unlike the taciturn and apathetic little girl she had been that the neighbors started wondering under their breath, in a collective murmur, if she wasn't a changeling switched by the Gypsies. Even though no one could remember exactly what Madre Lorenza Casado had written on that piece of paper, the word "genius" continued to resonate for a long time in the mouths of the entire family, to the point that each of them soon found Voltairean strokes of wit in the stream of childish words she babbled.

As well as studying every spare minute, Ana María cleared the table with Mama Concha until the last fork was washed, and took a dinner tray up to Tía África, who had remained cloistered in the back room since the death of her cousin Lina. She revealed herself to be a good adviser in the love troubles of Carmela Ramos del Valle, the cook who was exhausted from waiting for a husband to arrive in the bubbles of her dish-soap suds. She took part in the card games of Don Rafael Barroso, who confused the colors, and volunteered every Saturday of the month to cut the beard of Papapa, her aunt's husband, who still wore his old military uniform from the time of the dictator Gómez. She learned the poems by Doña Elvirita, to whom no one listened when she recited them in a Spanish that sounded as if it was borrowed from Machado, and developed the habit of reading the obituaries in *El Panorama*, for she lived in a house with so many old people that she was sure to find a death of someone they had known.

Soon she was never seen in public other than irreproachably groomed, perfumed, and coiffed, powdered even in those places that light never reached, her eyelids dusted with thyme, with that discrete elegance that is to be found among the poor, who are not rich enough to allow themselves to be badly dressed.

In those days there was a high school, the Colegio Sucre, that had been founded at the intersection of the Calle Ciencias and the Avenida Guayaquil by some women educators from Puerto Rico. Those courageous ladies, whose tenacity was reminiscent of the audacious and patient approach of missionaries, had brought from the islands an improbable innovation: giving girls an education equivalent to that given to boys. Going door to door loaded down with canvas bags full of textbooks, attempting to prove to reluctant mothers and severe fathers the unsuspected advantages of educating their daughters, they invited the parents to visit the school, which was an elegant, palatial two-story edifice in nineteenth-century architectural style, with wide arcade corridors and a marble frontispiece engraved with a line from the poet Marcial Hernández, under which one might still see men passing by in carts filled with sugarcane to be thrown under the grindstone of a mill.

But the tuition was expensive and Chinco could not afford this luxury. The headmistress of the Colegio, however, the very distinguished Doña Rafaela Capo de Alsina, who was called Missia Alcina, asked Chinco to come to her office one day and swept away all financial obstacles by assuring him that she was prepared to offer his daughter a scholarship.

"A woman must get an education, señor."

When Chinco came home that evening, while Ana María was reading in the living room, he set down on the table some signed papers and two blouses embroidered with the logo of the Colegio Sucre.

"You are enrolled in high school," he said to Ana María. "I couldn't help it. That Missia Alcina put a revolver to my heart."

Ana María thus went from a convent of inflexible nuns to a coeducational school where a grandmother named Carmelita Ortega de Finol played classical tunes in the classrooms on an old piano she wheeled from room to room. Each subject was taught by a different teacher, which was in contrast with the old system where all lessons were given by the same schoolteacher, but moreover Missia Alcina had the idea of encouraging the best students to participate in the competition organized by Professor Córdoba and the El Metro movie theater.

It was at that time, in October, that Ana María first met Antonio Borjas Romero, still a simple young man like so many others, a student at the federal high school, who bested her in a jousting match. He told her, "I hate going to the movies by myself."

And she would never have imagined that this boy whose name she did not know, a boy who was older than her and had sprung from the entrails of poverty, a boy who was more remarkable for the softness of his eyes than for his conqueror's face, would soon set down on her knees a notebook full of love stories and propose that she accompany him into the stormy mountains of desire, into a land where lovers die in each other's arms. She had no idea that he would be present in her most intimate battles, that their names would forever figure side by side on the porticos of Venezuelan medicine, that this young man who appeared to her to be rough and impertinent would also be the one to give her the greatest moments of tenderness, in her darkest hours, when Ana María, exhausted and alone, would decide to give up her fight. But all of this would occur much later. For now, Ana María would have kept only a hazy memory of Antonio were it not for a secondary event that came to project her destiny against his.

These were times of political unrest. Venezuela was living under the dictatorial regime of Juan Vicente Gómez. There were persecutions, arrests, detentions, and torture.

The halls of the San Carlos castle, where three centuries earlier the pirate Henry Morgan had managed to negotiate a ransom for the sixteen cannons in the fort, had been transformed into a labyrinth of dank cells and dungeons. A progressive group of students had created a political movement, the Federación de Estudiantes de Venezuela (FEV), to organize clandestine meetings and information networks founded by young leaders, including Rómulo Betancourt who would later become the president of Venezuela. Chinco had always been a socialist, and as the typographer of the Táchira railways, he put his printing presses at their disposal to publish a revolutionary communiqué that was circulated throughout the whole town. One of his colleagues, recognizing the seal of the organization, denounced him to the management: "Chinco Rodríguez should be locked up."

The following day, late in the morning, the police knocked insistently at the door in Calle San José to arrest him. Without waiting for a response, they broke through the latch with a kick and searched for Chinco in every room. He had been warned during the night by a loyal friend who was also part of the clandestine resistance.

In their sudden agitation, the policemen turned over the furniture, emptied the drawers, pulled down shelves, inspected under the beds, looking for any possible clue. After a thorough search, the regime's police found in his room only an empty bed, drawers with no clothes in them, and a slip of paper on his bedside table bearing the words: "The day of the revolution will come."

Chinco went into hiding on a farm not far from El Rodeo where chickens laid eggs twice a day and cockatoos landed on the pigs' backs. From there he was able to send coded letters that were later delivered with the greatest possible discretion to the house on Calle San José. Ana María waited for them with febrile impatience. Mama Concha was the only one able to decipher her son's illegible handwriting and would read them aloud in front of all the old people gathered together, hiding her tears and stumbling over the crossed-out phrases. Ana María asked her for the letters so she could keep them in a shoebox, and in the evenings she would go over them again with such nostalgia that in the end she knew them as well as if she had written them herself. No one ever heard her say anything untoward about the regime of Juan Vicente Gómez, not even when the missives became less and less frequent, nor when the dictatorship tightened its noose on clandestine activities. Nevertheless, this absence was formative in their relationship, and at that time, Ana María's feelings for her father turned into a reverence and admiration close to a mad crush.

The veneration she felt for him was unconditional. She started worshipping him like an idol. To listen to her, one would think she was trying to canonize him before his death. She repeated the sayings he had uttered, her gestures replicated his, and the image of that father had become not only a memory she adored but also an oracle she consulted.

Another year was drawing to a close, and Ana María realized that she had not given any thought to what she would do afterward. She knew nothing, neither about the world nor about herself, for it was her father who had always been concerned with her future, and beyond a few innocent dreams, she had never even considered leaving Maracaibo before that morning in June.

Ana María was seventeen at the time. She was studying her subjects with assiduity and discipline, when, one morning around nine in the corridors of the Colegio Sucre, she noticed the figure of a woman with fair hair and green eyes, who seemed to have appeared from a distant world of violins and brutality. This was Lya Imber de Coronil. She came from Ukraine. A pediatrician in Caracas, she had decided to travel the country, from one high school to the next, to encourage girls to study medicine, crisscrossing these tropical lands her family had adopted after their exodus, a wounded and courageous figure from a vanished world, who had fled the violence of antisemitism in Odesa and had embarked on a voyage to this continent that was still called the Occidental Indies, where women were believed to cut off their right breast to shoot better with a bow and arrow. Missia Alcina introduced her to the class.

"This is the first woman doctor of Venezuela."

The girls' febrile astonishment and the spellbinding impression the doctor made under their subjugated gaze was something Ana María never forgot. Nor did she ever forget the moment, in the incredible silence that fell once Carmelita had played her last notes on the piano, when the pediatrician, standing on the platform at the front of the class in her white coat, with her hair pulled back into a chignon, told them in her Slavic accent, without exaggerating or inventing anything, about her adventures in the vast continent of medicine. Ana María listened to her with such attention that she felt as if she was hearing a new language, the language of the future, which only women could understand. She tried to imagine those unexplored plains, to calculate the number of monstrous perils, to evaluate the obstacles to be surmounted and the tasks to be undertaken in order to impose herself in this kingdom built by men so far from God, and yet she felt the secret desire to resemble her. She examined the doctor's face, which appeared to belong not to a woman but to an evangelic creature, and she tried to understand how the profession's wildcats and barbarous jungles had not yet devoured her. And when Ana María returned home that night, she was resolved. She stood steadily in front of Mama Concha and had not the slightest trembling in her voice: "I shall be the first woman doctor of Zulia."

This decision, taken under the impulse of these expeditions and intrepid discoveries, came as a great surprise to the family. No one had ever heard of a woman doctor. Nevertheless, no one in the house on Calle San José was in any doubt that Ana María was a genius, since that day when the nun Lorenza Casado had written it on a slip of paper, as if she had engraved it on the frontispiece of her destiny, and it was decreed that if the Virgin Mary could bring a child into the world, then a poor girl from Maracaibo could wear a white coat. There was, however, no university in the town. She would need imperatively to go to Caracas. Chinco, who was still exiled on his farm, hiding out to avoid going to prison, could not send any money.

That is when the eleven old people in the house on Calle San José put together a pool of funds for Ana María's journey. Within a few days, all of them magically brought out ancient banknotes and silver objects, little saints' medals and family earrings, bracelets shaped like moons and rings that no fingers had worn for a hundred years, gold chains and even a Chinese jar decorated with slender cranes and giant stags of which no one knew the origins or how it happened to be there. Mama Concha, gathering it all together, was surprised at the fortune that had been drowsing in her own house and to the end of her days could never get over the idea that she had been sleeping on such a treasure for so long. It was Mama Concha who went on the journey with Ana María. Although she suffered from high blood pressure, arthritis in her knees, digestive troubles, and sciatica, she reassured everyone with a word: "What could possibly happen to me? I'll be traveling with this country's greatest woman doctor."

On June 12th, Ana María and Mama Concha left the house on Calle San José with eight trunks of clothes and dishes, parasols and suitcases of books, and a little gilded iron cage with a saffron-colored chaffinch who sang to announce the rain. They crossed Lake Maracaibo on a canoe to reach the port of La Ceiba in the south, sitting on wooden benches for the entire voyage that lasted two days, and from there traveled up the ancient trans-Andean road, which had been built twenty years previously with pickaxes, following the same path that Núñez de Balboa had taken in the other direction during the Spanish conquest, long ago, when he was searching for the southern sea.

The road went through almost no villages and crossed no other pathways. They boarded an old train called El Troller that took them, after a six-hour journey, to the crossroads of Motatán, a little village of mechanics and yucca saleswomen in the highlands of the state of Trujillo, where the first freeway going to Caracas started. At the intersection of the Andean paths, next to a gas pump lost in the middle of the plain, sunk into the ground and covered in dust, next to which a few sunburned motorbikes were standing in a silent line, they waited for a bus from the ARC company to take them to Barquisimeto, a twelve-hour trip.

The next day, after sleeping in a seedy hotel, they found a car that, ten hours later, dropped them off, exhausted by this odyssey, famished, and a thousand years older, on the Plaza la Candelaria, where Aura Josefina Rodríguez, the niece of a cousin of the first husband of her grandmother and a woman they had never met, was waiting for them.

This tiresome journey was, however, like a liquor of new worlds for Ana María. For all her seventeen years and the greedy curiosity of her youth, her provincial mind could not quite yet find its way in this profusion of images and stories, but her heart could already sense, behind this city of a hundred churches, universities as vast as forests filled with foreign students, hospitals with great white portals haunted by the ghosts of the wars of independence and of red-starred nights. She could not easily imagine any other city than this one in which to become a doctor, for this was where Lya Imber de Coronil had set out for, from beyond the Black Sea ports, to seek out not success nor recognition but an army of women.

Two months later, she entered the university. Ana María would remember for the rest of her life her first day in the lecture theater of the School of Medicine, across from the Congress building and next to the Church of San Francisco, an edifice covered in turrets which was a former monastery of Franciscan friars. She would never forget Doctor Pepe Izquierdo, the famous cardiologist, who had a reputation for coldness and implacable authority, and whom the students of every cohort continued to fear even after graduation. He was a tall thin man with hoary white hair, always dressed in a suit and tie with a gray rabbit-fur felt fedora on his head, and a pocket watch attached by a gold chain, which he consulted with a detached air. From the platform, as glacial as a rock, draped in a white coat that hung to mid-thigh, he had started sketching skeletons on the slate blackboard when suddenly, sweeping over the lecture theater with his eyes, he noticed her presence, that of a woman, and his eyes filled with contempt.

"Does your mother not have any more laundry to iron, señorita?"

All the men in the room laughed. Then he added, "You want to be a doctor? Well then, tell me the names of the seven bones of the orbit."

Ana María had never even heard of the orbit. She blushed so deeply she had to lower her head. Years later, remembering those mocking laughs around her, she understood that she had then felt something new palpitating inside her, her combative blood. Lineages of sleeping women had suddenly awoken in her veins, the bloody dagger of María Lionza riding a giant tapir, the bow and arrows of the queen of the Amazons, the dignity of Ana María Campos, the cropped hair of Agnodice, the heroic martyrdom of Domitila Flores, hordes of horsewomen galloping toward the fortresses of yesterday. She understood that she had a double battle to wage, for medicine and for women. She grasped how it would not be possible for her to go to inns and bars like everyone else, how she would not be allowed any errors, how she had no other option but to succeed, but she understood more than anything that the inexhaustible power of knowledge, the fortifying character of science would also help her to prevail.

The first months, as she expected, she endured affronts connected with her sex. Some of the male students crowded around her to whisper insults and lewd puns in her ears. She once discovered in her handbag a male organ that had been cut from a cadaver during an anatomy class. In the hospital canteen, there was a chair that had a hollow in its seat. One morning, some students filled it with urine and when she came in, presented it to her so she could sit down. Ana María was so annoyed that she protested ferociously, and this incident reached the ears of the rector, who called her into his office.

"Can you give me the name of this student?"

But Ana María kept her wits about her.

"I crossed the whole country to come study at this university," she replied. "I am not here to denounce my classmates."

On the twenty-sixth of every month, a box would arrive from Maracaibo with dresses made by her aunts; a bottle of wine to celebrate the *onomástico*, Santa Ana's day; and a box of fashionable shoes chosen at Santa Bárbara del Zulia by Chinco, who was looking after her from his exile. Ana María would wear only dresses with ribbons and a bow at the back and pajamas made of Bangladesh silk, which she kept on all night with delicate care. Despite the tenacious discipline with which she followed her classes, solitude had entered her life. Those first few weeks of isolation in the capital had made her long for the joyous and kindly troops in the home she had left.

She resolved to find new people and settled into a boardinghouse managed by the family of Don Leonidas Páez, a fine house near the Guanábano bridge, which took in students from the provinces who had no contacts in Caracas.

She never forgot that day either, when she found a flock of studious young men from all four corners of Venezuela, from which stood out a twenty-five-year-old man, with self-assured feline manners, wearing a light guayabera, a wide white linen shirt, with an anatomy textbook under his arm, who immediately approached her before she even had time to set down her suitcases.

"I hope you brought the notebook of love stories with you."

She immediately recognized the young man she had competed with a few years earlier in Professor Córdoba's classroom for the ticket to El Metro movie theater. Antonio was standing before her, right there, with a wide smile on his lips. They had not seen each other since the morning when she was sitting quietly under a tree and he had given her a notebook filled with a thousand love stories, but this time they immediately understood that a chance of rebirth, of new affinities, of a silent and invisible harmony was being offered to them. A few months in the bustling anthill of Caracas and the university had made them aware of the difficult situation of students from the provinces, who knew nothing of the unspoken rules of the capital nor its agitation, aware also of the harshness of being a stranger in one's own country. This allowed them to rediscover what had started between them in Maracaibo, but which had not until then had the time to crystallize.

Antonio had become a man. He was stronger and more handsome, even though the lines of his face had kept some of his childhood features. He still had the rosy complexion of the little tobacco seller, doll-like cheeks, and a roguish air, but when an idea crossed his mind, all it took was a second, the time of a lightning flash, for this face to transform itself into that of a giant. He carried the scent of the earth he had left behind, of the horses from the towpaths, of the reeds bathed in sunlight on the lagoon where, long ago, their common ancestors had erected their villages on stilts to resist the Spanish. He smelled of mangroves and bulls' horns, of the petroleum of the plains, and his accent reminded her of that abandoned world where the hills whispered the memories of fallen caciques buried with their weight in gold and where the tortoises' shells were covered in diamonds. From that day forward, Ana María always looked into his eyes to find the reflection of Lake Maracaibo.

That first year in medical school was also the first of their life together. They never noticed their seven-year age difference. Since there was only one microscope in the boardinghouse at Guanábano bridge, they used it together, taking turns lying face down on the floor, tenderly shoving each other to examine the slides, then discussing the forests of crystals and red suns whose infinite glow seemed to pass through the lens and visit them like an immortal secret. Some afternoons, they did not study but chatted until evening, walking a thousand times around the square or along the tracks that went up toward El Ávila. Ana María loved sitting on the steps of the church of the pantheon, to feel the presence of the sacred, to guess who the people were in the cloisters. She never let go of Antonio's arm, and as they sat on that step, he kept quiet about his origins and his birth, more out of tactfulness than shame.

This was how they started their second year, when they studied topographic anatomy with Professor Rivas Morales, using cadavers that the school borrowed from the morgue, on which they learned to recognize clinical pathologies. The third and fourth years were conducted in part at Vargas Hospital, where each student was assigned four patient beds, under the supervision of the head of the department, so that they could closely follow the evolution and treatment of an illness. Then came courses in semiology, bacteriology, parasitology, and the pharmacology of tropical diseases with professors who, like the princes of ancient societies, were able to give the details of their genealogy over several generations of physicians and to furnish the legends of their ancestors with anecdotes they had first heard as infants in their cradles.

In front of those professors, Antonio and Ana María did not dare divulge the modesty of their origins. They invented family histories for themselves that were full of conquests and sacrifices, on the other side of the country "beyond the lake" they said, telling stories of fathers who were cardiologists, and grandfathers who were as well, along with their great-grandfathers too, and they courageously ascended those chimeric and fictitious lineages in Maracaibo to the roots of this family profession in order to claim some share of legitimacy.

Ana María did her internship at the Concepción Palacios maternity clinic, attending deliveries and caesareans, plunging into a succession of curettages of the uterus, forceps, and manual extractions of placentas. Antonio, for his part, spent his at the Red Cross in Caracas, at the Carlos J. Bello hospital, on call three nights a week, such that he spent almost two years without seeing the light of day.

One September 27th, they were awarded their diplomas in medicine summa cum laude, during a magnificent soiree at the Paraninfo of the Central University of Venezuela, thus confirming the prophetic words that Don Victor Emiro Montero and Madre Lorenza Casado had pronounced about them.

Ana María and Antonio stayed a few more weeks in Caracas, living like fiancés. They wandered through the city hand in hand, kissing in the middle of the street without a care in the world. In the anonymity of the capital, they could imagine themselves living there, in the shelter of its protective crowd. But one morning, stirred by sudden nostalgia, Ana María awoke with a heavy head and turned to Antonio, whispering, "Now we have to go home."

As Antonio was not reacting, she leaned toward his ear and added, "We still have a story to write."

They took the same trans-Andean route home as Ana María had traveled with Mama Concha six years earlier, in the conviction that travelers' tales spoke the truth. As the bus was rocking them to sleep with the jolts from its wheels, Ana María closed her eyes and fell into a silent slumber, her head resting on Antonio's shoulder.

While the bus rolled through the jungle of Choroní, she had a strange dream of a black *tara*, a giant moth, which alighted on her father's neck. Its wings covered the landscape, and she did not see the kapok trees with their trunks flowing like wooden waterfalls, where the toucans hid their beaks of a thousand colors, nor the thickness of the carpet of ferns where a female ocelot was giving birth with a roar, nor the sloth with its thick fur, nor the vegetational walls of jacarandas and carob trees, nor the chameleon masticating an insect as big as a horsefly, she did not distinguish the fields of red and purple corn, which have the colors of the eye of the sunset, nor the impenetrable canopies of leaves that resembled the rose windows of cathedrals.

Antonio turned to look at Ana María. He saw her as no one ever had, so defenseless, so vulnerable, so abandoned to her dream, without her mask of courage and empowered womanhood, alone on earth. He felt he knew her already, or that they were so alike that he had met her in another lifetime. He recognized himself in that hidden fear, in that strength full of failings, and he felt at that instant a confidence in the future that made him shiver. With a cautious gesture, so as not to disturb her sleep, he tucked a lock of her hair behind her ear, caressed her temple, then placed his hand on her warm belly where he thought he could feel, between two lurches of the bus, the child yet to be born, waiting in the cotton wool of foretelling, the child who would come only later to give this couple moments of grandeur and heartbreak.

The bus stopped suddenly in the middle of the jungle, at El Venado. It must have been around 7:00 a.m. Two soldiers entered and went down the rows of seats.

"Is there someone called Ana María Rodríguez here?"

"That's me," she said as she stood up. "What's happening?"

"Follow us."

She took Antonio's hand and replied forcefully, "I'm not going anywhere without him."

"He can come if you wish."

They got off the bus and were accompanied to an elegant black Cadillac with tinted windows. Inside, a smiling man in a suit opened the door and had them sit down.

"What's happening?" Ana María repeated.

"What is happening, Señora Rodríguez, is that the governor has sent me to collect you. The state of Zulia cannot allow the first woman physician to enter Maracaibo in a vulgar bus, *doctora*."

Ana María's eyes widened in surprise. It was the first time that anyone had called her *doctora*. She turned to Antonio, who shrugged in stupefaction.

"You will be welcomed on Plaza Bolívar," the man said.

Plaza Bolívar was then the hottest square in the world. In the middle of the afternoon, women waited for the bus in the lines of shade provided by the electrical poles and men fried eggs on the hoods of cars. Rumor had it that prisoners would exchange their most humiliating chores for an ice cube to put on the back of their necks and that the reverberation of the sunlight deformed the metal of the prison bars. The heat was so stifling there that even at night people thought it was still daytime. The businesses, the schools, the bazaars, the lottery shops, everything shut down shortly before noon and only opened again after four o'clock, when the shade grew wider.

That was why, on November 14th at around three o'clock, everyone was surprised to see a gathering of elected dignitaries, town hall employees, and all the local press. The heat had reached its daily peak when a parade of official cars appeared on the avenue, in the middle of which one could see, through the windows of an armored four-wheel drive, driven by the governor's personal chauffeur, a woman who looked like an exhausted high-school student.

For the space of an instant, the ice-cream sellers and the passersby removed their sunglasses to look more closely at the features of this young woman being brought into the square with great pomp, with her little braids circling her head, holding her books and wearing a cotton dress of the simplest cut. Someone raised their voice to say that she was probably the president's wife. The governor himself, through a microphone that had been installed on a stage, explained the situation by declaring that the city wished to bid Ana María Rodríguez welcome.

"She is the first woman doctor of the state of Zulia," he said with pride. "And she comes from Maracaibo."

He gave her his arm and escorted her down to a street that had been decorated with pots of gardenias and colored flags, in a deafening concert of trumpets and friction drums. The inhabitants of Maracaibo, who had never seen a woman precede a man in public before, rushed to their balconies and windows, convinced that they were witnessing a historic event. Ana María, disoriented by this hullabaloo, exhausted by the journey, did not get involved in the ceremony. When the governor leaned toward her ear to announce that she was about to be decorated with the city's medal, she was not moved.

"I just want to go home."

On the threshold of her house, arms lifted her off the ground. Her father Chinco came to greet her, and their reunion was a shower of kisses. Exile had aged him and caused him to lose weight. However, the youthful glow of his eyes had remained intact, and his daughter's return endowed him with renewed vigor.

"Ana María," he said, looking at her closely, "you are a genius."

Six years had passed since her departure for Caracas, but to look at her, anyone would think she had been gone for twenty. Her face had acquired the wisdom of adult life. Her gaze was no longer that of a little girl protected by her father, pampered by her family, raised like a princess, but had hardened into that of a woman. Her voice had changed. An entire city life of perseverance and challenge, of dignity and conquest, of secret pains and unexpected promises could be read in her calm and assured gestures.

The day after her arrival, on Monday at six-thirty in the morning, Ana María had already drunk her coffee when Chinco opened the windows looking out over the street. He had to clutch the sill in order not to fall over.

"Who are all these people?" he asked.

Ana María ran to the window and saw women of all ages, standing one behind the other in the crushing morning heat, carrying baskets of food and flower crowns, dressed in the simplest clothes, forming an extravagant procession in front of her house. The line stretched more than three blocks and lost itself behind the church. It was as if an army of women had surrounded her house in a deployment of dresses and parasols, a mobilization of worn-out fans and felt hats, all of them wishing to catch a glimpse of her, to stop and get a good look. The news had spread overnight beyond the outskirts of Maracaibo, all the way into the villages to the south of the lake where medicine was completely unheard of, and had provoked such a wave of excitement and agitation in the female population as had not been seen since the discovery of oil.

Ana María spent the entire day examining this interminable crowd, jotting down on a little card the days of their ovulations, according to the duty of her oath, but the procession was not thinning but even continuing to grow, for behind the last young women there would always be other seamstresses, laundresses, or cooks muttering prayers, dozens of women in failing health, who had grown thirsty from the long wait, their skin covered in scabs and their retinas burned by the sun. They brought tablecloths in boxes, horoscopes, and bunches of plantains, chaffinches with golden wings locked in cages, candles in the shape of cherubs, and glass jars full of preserved eggs. That was the description that Ana María herself later gave of the event, when she revisited the memory of her return to Maracaibo.

An old Argentinean Gypsy woman with jet-black hair who appeared one evening, singing milongas and drinking maté, read Ana María's future in the cards.

"You will soon have a son," she told her. "But he will not be of you or for you."

The Gypsy could say no more, for the clarity of the future had been blurred by the arrival of other people in the house. Ana María did not give much credence to this prophecy. The following days, there was a hail of articles in the press. She was invited to give speeches, seminars, presentations in schools, and a week later was appointed the head of a clinic of thirteen beds at the hospital of Nuestra Señora de Chiquinquirá, under the protective wing of Monsignor Aquiles Penazca, who blessed her scissors before her first operation.

Because there were no more new cars to be had since World War II, she bought an old secondhand one, a black Buick that had once belonged to the consul of the Netherlands and was now covered in rust, but which was one more step toward her freedom and independence, making her one of the first women of Maracaibo to get a driver's license. However, it would not be long before things turned sour, and the sparkling gold penguin brooch that Ana María proudly wore on her white coat was soon tarnished by the shadow of bereavement.

One morning as he was getting into Ana María's car, Chinco misjudged his movement and lightly banged his head against the rusty metal. Ana María smiled at his clumsiness and had no concern about this insignificant injury, for the wound was superficial and a small bandage was enough to contain the faint bleeding. But tetanus soon took hold of his body. This was during the period when the first sewers were being opened up in the city, infecting the air with spores and bacteria from the excrement of the horses and mules that were still used for transportation in the avenues. The following day, fire broke out in his veins, his jaw locked, his entire body stiffened like a wooden plank, and by the early hours of the morning, Chinco Rodríguez was no more than a ball of fire. He spent entire days in delirium, navigating through a swamp of nausea, his head the scene of a battle of giants, and Ana María thought she detected the abominable signs of madness.

At the time there were two doctors in Maracaibo who were malaria specialists, three dentists who imported canisters of laughing gas to anesthetize their patients, and forty-three shamans, along with thirteen therapists of the Holy Spirit who were never seen without branches of white poplar and strings of sandarac beads as they repeated the incantations in the Yoruba language they had learned from their ancestors, and whose expertise required no diplomas since it came to them directly from the unassailable universities of the African divinities. A healer from the sierra put a large black leech above the wound. It was thick and glossy, as long as a salamander, and started extracting the venom with such diabolical strength that it lost all its flesh, became a little dried-up slug as withered as a vanilla pod, and died eight hours later, exhausted from having sucked so much.

At the end of the week, when all the medicasters of the surrounding farms had come and gone by his bedside, proposing all sorts of drugs and bleeds with herbs, the only result was to make him lose the white of his eyes, leaving a yellowish color around his irises as if someone had poured cornmeal onto his cornea. Defeated, they resolved to commit this man into the hands of the Lord, for they were convinced that nothing and nobody could now stand between him and death. For his last night, Mama Concha served him a plate of grated fresh cheese, accompanied with a plantain sprinkled with cinnamon, and held up his head so he could swallow.

"You mustn't die on an empty stomach," she told him.

At dusk, as he lay on his bed of palm fronds and had lost all hope of recovery, he learned that Ana María had found a tetanus specialist in Caracas who was on his way to Maracaibo. But he was never able to meet this man, for at that very moment death came to claim him in the shape of a *tara* the color of night, a moth called a black witch, as big as a bat with outstretched wings, which had wedged itself in the corner of the ceiling one rainy Friday, leading everyone to understand that José "Chinco" de la Chiquinquirá, the typographer from Calle San José, would not survive the night. On June 24th, one hundred and twenty-three years after the Battle of Carabobo, at three in the morning, Mama Concha was awoken by a death rattle in the bedroom and found the nightstand lamp tipped over, the sheets on the floor, books scattered all over the ground, and in the middle of this catastrophe, his mouth open and his eyes empty, Chinco Rodríguez stretched out on his belly with the black *tara* sitting on the nape of his neck.

A vigil was held for him in the house on Calle San José. From Plaza Bustamante to the cemetery, flowers rained down on the crowd that came to see his grave. Because he'd had progressive and anticlerical ideas, a religious service and Christian ceremony was not deemed appropriate, but there was nevertheless a desire to organize a funeral worthy of his renown by bringing in a man of faith. When Monsignor Aquiles Penazca arrived in the living room, he had to make a pathway through the crowd by moving people aside with his wooden cross, elbowing through the throng, to reach the honorable remains of that old socialist, killed by the rust of the world, shriveled up by the last days of convulsions, his complexion pale and waxy, his body surrounded by a halo of jasmine and dried pomegranates. He was exhibited to the sight of all comers, in the middle of the living room, next to a table on which his typographer's tools were displayed, and for the three days that the vigil lasted, no one dared ask the whereabouts of Ana María.

The first few nights, Ana María did not leave her bed and cried until she lost her voice. No one could even imagine how this bereavement had ravaged her. Her sobs could be heard from Calle San José to Plaza Baralt, and even the throngs of people who had invaded the house bringing presents, even the *gaita* concert given as a farewell to Chinco from the sidewalk, even the rumbling of the neighbors coming and going in the living room could not drown out her cries of pain.

Three days later, Ana María came out of her room. Sadness had deformed her face and even her own mother could not recognize her. From that day forward, she was in such strict mourning that she no longer opened the shutters on her windows and forbade everyone from saying her father's name if she was not present. She dressed him, combed his hair, crossed his hands over his chest, and it was with her tears that she washed his forehead for the last time. Before the body was put into the coffin, she ordered a mortuary mask of gray plaster to be made, the coarse features of which bore no resemblance to the fineness of his face, but on which no one dared to comment, for Ana María was convinced that this portrait had managed to capture the eternity of his expression. In the middle of the night, still lost in slumber, she would take it out of its sheepskin case and contemplate it in the darkness. It seemed to her to glow in the dark.

She had all the lightbulbs in the house changed so that the indoor lighting was less intense, under the pretext that the light of her life had been extinguished, and she saw the semidarkness she had established around her as a fertile ground for communicating with the spirit world. She spoke with the dead through a medium and held séances after dinner. One evening when Ana María had invited the sorcerer Babel Bracamonte into the living room and he had arrived with chalk sticks to draw triangles on the floor and to light cigars of black tobacco, Antonio put an end to these diabolical practices.

"Your father is dead," he said. "If you want to bring him back to life, save other lives."

For a few days she remained silent, holding back her tears and chasing away bad thoughts. One morning, as if she had woken up from this lethargy, she resolved to empty her father's room to get rid of not just his things but also the burden on her own heart. Tía África would long remember that morning when Ana María entered Chinco's old room and, without opening the shutters at the windows, in the darkness of her pain, started sorting everything, putting it in order, throwing things out, until his evocation was no more than a pile of papers and cardboard boxes smelling of bougainvillea.

It took four mornings to get everything out. In the end, this therapy proved miraculous. Ana María regained her old strength. When the room was empty, before she left, she had a suspicion that something was still in there. Ana María sensed that her father had hidden a treasure somewhere in his house, more personal, intimate objects.

As she tapped along the baseboards, she discovered a pinewood box hidden behind a loose slat, a delicately carved little casket the size of a shoe carton, in which he had concealed his secrets from prying eyes. It was closed up like an Indian tomb, sealed by prayers and spirit sentinels, and when she opened it, she found the interior covered in dark red velvet. Inside it was a gold nail and a dried rabbit's foot, a lock of her hair and a few family necklaces. Her eyes were attracted to the bottom of the box, where there was a piece of paper folded into four, which she immediately recognized.

It was the note from Madre Lorenza Casado, who had declared many years ago that Ana María was a genius. Her father had kept it in this box for twenty years. She felt her throat tighten. When she unfolded it, Ana María read the following words: “Your daughter is an idiot. She has nothing to do in this institution. Educate her at home.”

After the death of Chinco Rodríguez, Ana María and Antonio settled in the heart of Avenida 3H, a few yards from the Plaza de la República, in a large house where the light flowed in like waterfalls. It was a simple construction bearing the name Ilusión, which Antonio rebaptized Quinta Ana María. There were five bedrooms, furniture of olive wood carved with patterns of jellyfish, and porcelain tile floors. At the back of the house was a tropical courtyard with blue-painted pavers surrounded by monsteras and rubber trees, which led out onto the street where Ana María smoked a pipe of dark tobacco and hummed love songs in the evenings. From that spot she could see the bell tower of the cathedral of Chiquinquirá and the roof of the Teatro Baralt, the tip of the sword of Simón Bolívar on his bronze horse and on clear days, farther off in the distance, the faint silhouctte of the port from which the customs ships with their Panama flags departed.

The first night, at around eleven, it was not the mosquitoes that woke Antonio but a cavernous rasping that seemed to be coming from inside his own bedroom. He tried to go back to sleep. The lament came back twice more, then at the third groan, Antonio shook his wife awake to warn her that there seemed to be someone crying under their bed. Ana María, still half asleep with her back turned, reassured him without even opening her eyes.

"It's probably just someone who died in this room long ago," she said. "Give them a few days. It'll pass."

To stop hearing the deceased, Antonio had a four-poster bed built, with folding panels that could be shut at night, and four elephant feet in sterling silver, each of which was heavier than the bed itself. He covered the walls with mirrors to open up the room and reflect the light, but also to keep an eye on all the comings and goings, such that it was impossible to move anywhere in the house without being seen in a reflection. Ana María hired a driver and two cleaning ladies who went through every room with a fine-tooth comb daily, leaving behind in the air a strong smell of sawdust and Creolina disinfectant. But although Ana María and Antonio had arranged everything so they could live like princes, they did not spend much time at home. During this period there was a great deal of agitation at the hospital, and they were pulled between their love of hospitality and their work.

"Come whenever you like," they said. "We are never at home anyway."

While Ana María was working at the Nuestra Señora de Chiquinquirá clinic, wearing four rows of fine pearls around her neck and a diamond solitaire on her finger even during the most difficult deliveries, Antonio, who had his white coats stiffened with cornstarch, set up a practice in Calle Carabobo that had a nocturnal emergency service.

One evening, a woman came into his practice, accompanied by a young boy. Antonio, who was finishing writing a letter, was so concentrated on his task that he asked her to sit down without raising his eyes. When she was settled in front of him, he glanced quickly at her face. A familiar look suddenly aroused his attention, captivating features that reminded him of someone without him being able to say of whom. He stared at her.

"You don't remember me then, *hombrecito*?" she asked with a smile.

He did not immediately recognize Leona Coralina, the prostitute with the shaved head from the Majestic, for she had lost her provocative youth with such speed that it seemed she had never known it. He found her more faded than in his recollection, with traces of sadness in her eyes.

He straightened up and apologized. "How could I forget you?" he cried, then embraced her with a mixture of friendship and modesty, all under the child's gaze. She was obese, downcast, and exhausted; there was not much left of the frisky panther she had once been in the darkness of the bedrooms at the Majestic, of the legendary siren whose name resounded all the way from Maicao to Barbados, of those Homeric locks that a governor had once paid for in land titles, and he realized that he had completely forgotten this woman for years, since that long-ago day when, one morning in May, she had thrown herself on his adolescent body with blind passion.

"Allow me to introduce Oscar," she said, indicating the twelve-year-old boy at her side.

He was much too tall for his age. Oscar had thick black eyebrows that made a bridge over his nose, and rough features hardened by an inner rage that already marked his face as that of an adult. A scar cut his chin in two, from his lower lip to his neck, dividing the bottom of his face, and when he smiled, a valley of skin slowly opened up with the softness of wax. He was born in the sumptuous times of the first Majestic, of an unknown father, and from this mother who had slept with all the men in the world. The birth of this child had marked Leona Coralina's body severely. The skin of her belly had turned brown and soft like a dead leaf, her breasts had been emptied by the insatiable gargantuan appetite of this young colossus, her hips had doubled in size during the delivery, and Antonio understood, without her having to say a word, that this unjust destiny of her body had made her lose her hegemony in the house of Lucrecia Montilla.

At forty, she was forced to renounce the oldest profession in the world to sell figurines of the Virgin at the doors of churches. She had found a refuge of peace in religion, and the day when she started feeling strong pains on the right side of her lower abdomen, like a dagger stuck into the hilt, not knowing anyone and with no idea where to go with her titanic child to care for, she asked God to light her way. That very evening, as she was wrapping her Virgins in newspaper, she saw Antonio's picture by chance in an article and recognized El Hombrecito, that orphan from Pela el Ojo who had become a doctor and bore no resemblance anymore to the timid boy she had known long ago during that distant period of the Majestic.

"Leona," said Antonio after examining her gently, "you have acute appendicitis."

She looked at him without understanding. "That's too bad," she replied.

"You need an operation, urgently," Antonio insisted.

Leona shrugged. "Never mind, *hombrecito*. I have no money."

Antonio swept away that sentence with the back of his hand. That morning of lovemaking eighteen years previously, and the common memory of their youth, saved Leona Coralina's life.

A few days later, when she was convalescing from the operation, her tears prevented her from thanking Antonio. It was her son who approached him. He was so tall that he was two heads higher than Antonio. He reached out an enormous hand, square and hard like the knot in a tree trunk, and Antonio then heard his voice: "Doctor Antonio Borjas Romero, I hope to be able to thank you one day man to man."

Leona Coralina's operation coincided with the beginning of the dictatorship of Marcos Pérez Jiménez. This was at the end of the 1940s. Ana María, who had been called by the Ministry of Health to become the honorary president of the Medical Institute of Assistance, realized what was happening the day she witnessed the arrest of a young male nurse at the hospital. No one had heard the truck of soldiers arrive. Armed men rushed in, yelling. Doors were kicked open, the sound of boots crashed through the halls, loud voices barked orders. Three soldiers broke into the operating room with a bestiality that made the walls shake and suddenly charged the air with the smell of gunpowder. They were tall and frightening in their dark glasses, khaki uniforms, and dirty brogans, and they immediately brought a climate of tension with them. Ana María ordered them to leave.

"No woman tells a man what to do," one of the soldiers replied.

They took away the young male nurse, and he was never seen again from that day forward. Ana María then understood that a terrifying minotaur had just emerged from the labyrinths under her country, which would not only darken the next ten years but also smash the serenity of her own life. Antonio, who was caught up in either the renovations to the house on Avenida 3H or the management of his emergency practice, was perhaps the last person to understand this. He had just been nominated to preside at the second surgery congress in Venezuela when Ana María pulled him out of his reverie by telling him he could do nothing without the agreement of the "little fat guy."

"Which little fat guy?" he asked in surprise.

"The new dictator," she replied.

Marcos Pérez Jiménez had hoisted himself into power in 1948 through a coup d'état, never suspecting that it would also be a coup that would dethrone him ten years later. He made the unions, the Communist Party, and all student movements illegal. There was an oil strike that was brutally quashed. The newspaper *Tribuna Popular* denounced the political prisoners of El Dorado; it was closed down.

Ana María and Antonio could see the abrupt change in the country. Three years after the start of the dictatorship, a widespread unease started affecting all the social classes in Venezuela. And at the very moment when plans were being laid for the longest bridge on the continent to span the lake, to connect the two shores and the capital with Zulia, which would remain in memory as a wonder of engineering of nearly nine thousand yards and one hundred and thirty-four pillars, the workers and farm laborers, who had neither rights nor land, saw their incomes plummet. Students were humiliated, persecuted, put on trial. Never before in all the political history of the country had this kind of repression been known, such that it was said that not a leaf moved on a tree without the dictator being told about it.

"We have to do something," Antonio had said to Ana María one evening, "but what?"

While Maracaibo was reduced to silence and gagged by censorship, Ana María spent long hours at the maternity clinic examining patients, attending births, caring for each woman, without eating or drinking, completely devoted to her vocation. She barely left the hospital to get some sleep at home. She forgot herself so much that she lost twenty pounds in a few months and the clothes that she had worn since her glorious student days in Caracas were soon too big for her. The long night shifts erased the last traces of adolescence from her looks, and the daily pressure, exhaustion, and urgent cases that were added to her schedule laid down a sediment of distress in the depths of her eyes that made her facial features more severe. Worried about his wife's health, Antonio asked her to take it easy. Ana María replied, "Let us rest together. The world has gone mad."

And so, they decided to sit under their pergola and become strangers to the abhorrent rumors of the dictatorship gnawing at the country, and made love with the haste of those who have no thought for the morrow. Twenty years later, Ana María could easily go back to the memory of that time of inspiration and frenzy, when she threw herself at Antonio in the middle of the day in the hallways of their house, in the empty bedrooms at the back, and offered herself to him without protection, defying her bodily cycles.

When she became pregnant at the end of April 1957, she left the management of her clinic and resolved to spend the rest of her pregnancy alone at home, with the windows shut, so that no one could come between her and her child. Antonio learned the news a few days later.

He was coming home from the hospital one Tuesday morning after a long night shift and noticed that Ana María was in the garden, lying in a hammock, her belly covered in camellia stems and vanilla-tree bark.

"There will soon be three of us at home," she whispered.

Antonio felt his heart swell in his chest. He pointed toward the sky. "God will give us a boy," he said, "and he will be a cardiologist."

But Ana María replied very calmly, covering herself with a silk robe that she would not take off until the birth, "God has nothing to do with it. I want a girl."

Ana María dismissed the cook and the cleaning ladies, locked the front door, and thus spent the last few months of her pregnancy entirely alone in the middle of her large house. She moved around her back courtyard as through a garden of delights, wandering imaginary orchards with Akkadian slowness, dressed only in her tunic, while chewing raspberry leaves and urinating on barley grains whose rapid germination would indicate the imminent arrival of the child. She drifted wherever she pleased, whenever she pleased, noticing her thighs filling with water, her breasts with milk, and her hips widening. She felt as if she were about to deliver the first woman in the world.

Toward midday, when the sun was at its zenith, she would seek refuge in the coolness of her bedroom with its closed shutters and take four-hour siestas. She dreamed of her daughter's face, by combining her own features and Antonio's in her sleep, but at the cost of an enormous effort of imagination that obliged her to navigate through an ocean of babies that all blended together in her head, hundreds of faces she had delivered in the maternity clinic, and this dream was full of ships throwing their anchors into the future. She would then see the spirit of Chinco descend toward her from his messianic heights. She saw him whirling around the room like a *tara* in a glass cloche, flitting up to the sides without hitting them. She spoke to him about her daughter, about the destiny she had traced out for her, shivering with joys and fears, convincing herself that the breath of fresh air that slid between the blades of the shutters was an embrace that Chinco was sending to her as protection.

At the same time, near the end of 1957, a communiqué published by the College of Medicine of Caracas clandestinely arrived in Maracaibo accompanied by two doctors from the capital, Pino Rosales and Parra León. It was a call for disobedience and revolt. The two doctors contacted Antonio early in the morning and asked him, through a friend, whether he wished to rally to the cause. Antonio, who had seen the country crumble, censorship eat away at freedom of expression, and the parliament collapse, accepted.

Ana María, with her enormous belly, ready to give birth, joined up with Antonio. They braved the dangers together. In an urge as instinctive as the one that made them board a train to cross the country and become one of the most famous couples of Maracaibo, they enlisted in the rebellion against the dictatorship. They held secret meetings in clinics, hospitals, and maternity wards; led sessions, distributed information, facilitated connections between activists, hid combatants; and little by little, the taste for risk and resistance, which they had never really explored before, set their hearts ablaze. No one could suspect that this elegant couple expecting their first child organized the circulation of messages, moved money around from unknown sources, falsified names and dates, altered addresses and gathered evidence, all in the most profound clandestinity.

Ana María's pregnancy meant that she mostly stayed at home in the protective shadows. But Antonio's revolutionary activities gradually led him to become the head of the College of Medicine, which attracted the suspicion of the national police. He was rapidly identified by the secret services as one of the architects of a conspiracy dedicated to overthrowing the government, and it was not long before he was being tracked.

The word spread among the doctors that he was being pursued. He was hidden in Marxist haciendas, protected from prying eyes and rumors, until the day when the party was denounced and he had to flee to the north, toward Sinamaica, farther inland. At El Carmelo, he escaped a raid by soldiers on a warehouse where he had been hiding, and at Cuatro Bocas, he survived a shooting that broke out on a crocodile farm. Three weeks went by without Ana María having any news of him. Her due date was approaching. In such a terrifying situation, she was afraid that her anxiety would cause the baby to be born prematurely, and she had the bitter feeling of reliving that horrible period when her father was forced into exile, persecuted, and silenced, as if the history of men was nothing more than a slow loop indefinitely repeating itself.

Without telling anyone, Antonio came back to Maracaibo. No village can hide a man better than a city. Disguised as a consul, wearing gloves and a top hat, driving a very elegant Cadillac on loan from a friend, convinced that the safest place was between the wolf's jaws, he entered via the main street, protected by the crowds. But despite all these precautions, after a time hiding out in the D'Empaire clinic, he was found by the police in the second week of January, at one in the morning. He had been working very late after a meeting of union leaders when he saw an armed young soldier enter. The soldier ordered Antonio to follow him, but Antonio refused to get into a vulgar police wagon. He grabbed his leather briefcase with its silver handle, slid on his gloves, and donned his elegant top hat, and it was only when dressed as a dandy that he turned to the young soldier and, dangling the keys to his beautiful Cadillac parked at the entrance, declared in a resolute voice: "I will go in my own car. And you will follow me."

That is how he drove himself to the prison of the Cuartel Libertador, the main post office building that had been transformed into a dungeon, where he was interrogated that same evening.

"Tell us about that communiqué you circulated throughout the city."

"I do not know what you are referring to," Antonio replied.

The slap he received made him fall to the ground. He tasted blood in his mouth and the ringing in his right ear muffled the noise of the insults that the soldier was shouting as he leaned over him. Antonio noticed the soldier had a signet ring on one finger. He touched the wound where he had been hit, and understood that the ring had broken his eye socket. Since Antonio said nothing, one of the soldiers mocked him: "You're tough, are you? Let's see how long you can go on being clever with Amerigo. He's a madman."

Antonio did not see the kick that threw him against the wall. Then a shower of blows rained down on him and he felt as if there were ten of them beating him. They smashed his ribs. Folded over on the floor like a dog, unable to breathe, he protected his head with his arms. They grabbed him by the hair and punched his nose until blood spurted onto the tiles. He was crawling on the ground, wailing in pain, when he heard: "Take him to the *escuelita*."

The torture at the *escuelita* consisted of being detained for hours sitting on a wooden plank covered in little cut-off cones. Antonio suffered in silence, held firm, then all of a sudden felt the blood violently rush to his head until he lost consciousness. He woke up later, thrown in a heap at the back of a dank cell, his trousers torn, humiliated like a beaten dog.

During this first week of detention, while Ana María was writing hundreds of letters every day asking for his release, and while Paz Galarraga was continuing to fight in the highlands of the sierra, Antonio stayed in his cell filing his nails on the stone walls and repeating the names of the bones of the wrist so as not to lose his mind. As he recollected his past, he kept only the memory of that instant of irreducible joy when he first met Ana María in a classroom, surrounded by the other girls of Missia Alcina, and he wondered if he would ever know the child sleeping in her belly. During all this time, he had worked like a slave far away from home, busy with the exigencies of his career, and it had taken him fifteen years of winning all the prizes and being awarded all the distinctions of his profession to discover the superiority of love.

The following day, two armed men dressed in military uniforms came to drag him out like an animal and took him into a room for an interrogation.

"You're tough, are you? You don't talk? Let's see if you don't talk to Amerigo. He's crazy. Anyone who comes in here as a man ends up crying like a baby."

He was left alone for two hours in a cold room. Fear was rising in him. At last the door opened. A giant appeared in a frame of light. From the moment the torturer entered, Antonio felt intimidated by the phenomenal mass of his body, the brutal power that emanated from it, and the coldness in his eyes that made Antonio think that this man was capable of beating him to death. The soldier had just come from another room where he had caused an academic to lose consciousness during a session of unbelievable barbarity. His hands were still daubed with blood and tufts of hair. Antonio's face, plunged in the cell's darkness, only appeared in fragments, in poorly lit sections. But when the torturer approached and distinguished his face in brighter light, he seemed suddenly confused.

"Doctor Antonio Borjas Romero?"

Antonio was not surprised that he knew his name, only at the softness with which the question was asked.

"Yes," he said.

The torturer's eyes grew wide. He added in a slow voice, "You operated on my mother ten years ago and saved her life." He had to bite his lip and lower his eyes. "It is an honor to stand before you, doctor."

Antonio, who had kept his cool, examined the features of the torturer's face more carefully. Until then, he had not had the chance to look at him properly. He was surprised to see that the soldier's hands were shaking and noticed the scar on his chin. This barbaric giant was Leona Coralina's son. He remembered the courageous boy who had waited for his mother to recover in the hospital corridors with such touching patience, and had shaken his hand after the operation was over, then promised that they would see each other again someday.

"How is your mother doing?" Antonio asked.

"She left us in October."

Antonio whispered a "May she rest in peace," the torturer replied "Amen," and a fraternal silence fell between them, like a ceasefire in the aberration of the world, in honor of that Colombian woman whose hair had once provoked such delirious love in the Caribbean.

"What happened to us, doctor?" he asked.

Antonio puffed out his chest. "Do what you've come here to do. I don't have the time."

The torturer looked at him for a long time. He remained pensive, vacant, until he stood up.

"I never knew who my father was. But I would have wanted him to be you."

He turned on his heel and left. Antonio observed him leaving the cell and wondered how old the boy was. Days passed. Locked up, broken, discarded into oblivion, he felt time go by so slowly that he lost all track of it. Silence had spread over his life. A silence that forced him to remain speechless, to renounce everything. While he was getting used to this new destiny, convinced that he would spend the rest of his days incarcerated and scratching the stone walls with his fingernails, while he was imagining his wife's first contractions, the commotion of nurses running here and there, and the first cries of pain, Antonio could not suspect that the streets were also already preparing for their own deliverance.

He could not know that, on the outside, a thousand little events had started cracking the inviolable wall of the regime, that revelations were coming to light, that the masses were attempting to rise up, that the unions were organizing in the shadows, that the battle was reemerging from a buried world, and that everything was becoming agitated, bustling, that anything was possible.

On the morning of January 23, 1958, Antonio Borjas Romero, the *doctora* Ana María, and the dictator Marcos Pérez Jiménez woke up as if it was just another day in their lives, without suspecting that one would be freed in the afternoon, the other would lie down that evening with a baby girl in her arms, and the third would flee to a foreign country, destitute and isolated, after narrowly escaping execution.

That day in the back of his cell, Antonio was squashing the ants on his pillow when he heard the sound of car horns growing louder. He stopped, pricked his ears, held his breath to listen to this miracle more closely, for since the beginning of the dictatorship it was strictly forbidden to use a car horn. He suddenly understood that this was the voice of revolt. The people had risen up, anger and frustration had overflowed, the car horns were Maracaibo's call to battle. The first cries and first clashes erupted all over the city, yells and gunshots, trucks starting up at high speed, broken windows. Within a few hours, the atmosphere was filled with cracks and barking, with shocks and deflagrations, and Antonio believed he was hearing the symphony of insurrection.

At around midday, the same car horns reached Ana María's ears in her house on Avenida 3H and provoked sudden contractions.

"It will be today," she said calmly.

She was taken to the maternity clinic through the blazing streets. Stones and Molotov cocktails were flying, trash cans were burning, the crowds were being machine-gunned, a battle was raging. When Ana María arrived at the hospital, she had to go in through the emergency entrance, for youths had set fire to a gas pump and thrown it onto the main forecourt. It was a scene of complete chaos. At 3:00 p.m. the city went wild. The military school liberated its men, the commanders turned their coats, the army rose up against the dictatorship, and Marcos Pérez Jiménez was obliged to take flight in his private plane, the *Sacred Cow*, with such haste that he abandoned a suitcase full of dollars at the airport.

It was at that instant, when the dictator was at an altitude of ten thousand feet, saved just in time, that Ana María felt her pelvis rip apart ten thousand feet below. She disappeared from herself, was almost unconscious, suddenly assailed by a pinnacle of pain, and all that remained in the room, floating above the midwives and the nurses, was a scream sounding like a man being stabbed, a cry blending with that of the Venezuelan people who, at the same instant, were marching down the main avenue shouting, "The dictator has fallen! Viva Venezuela!"

The voice of the streets was so loud that after an hour no one could hear Ana María's agonized cries, for all the medical staff were agitated by the gunshots and explosions of joy coming from the front of the building that entered the delivery suite and announced, amid the spurting blood, the dawning of a new political era, a new departure, an origin yet to come. "Viva Venezuela," they cried. And this origin, it was Ana María who was thrusting it out of her belly.

She managed to grip the bars of the bed ferociously and to push with all her might. She could suddenly feel the head passing through and tearing her inner walls, "Viva Venezuela," she felt that head entering the rich hours of the history of a continent, emerging into the tumult of the streets, she felt that head leading her up through the centuries of Latin America, to the Spanish conquest and colonialist heritage of the masters of the valley, to the empires of Indigenous priests and the archaic dynasties, "Viva Venezuela," that head passing through the maritime battles in the gulf, recollecting the oldest memories of its societies, traveling up the course of rivers to the geological times of mineral warfare, from the primitive splendor of a first lizard peeking its nose out of a prehistoric shell, "Viva Venezuela," and Ana María, who was pushing from the underground limestone sediments, felt such intense pain that it took her even further, into the time when there were no rocks nor sand, no oppressors nor oppressed, no daybreak nor devotion, but only, suspended in the middle of nothingness, the magnificent void of a first star.

"What name do you wish to give your child?" the nurse asked.

Ana María was about to reply when Antonio burst into the delivery suite. He had been freed in the chaos and jumped through a broken window, then had to run barefoot through the catastrophe, over shards of glass and the embers of fires; he had galloped across the city like one possessed and rushed breathlessly up the stairs. He was two minutes late.

The newborn was already in her mother's arms, her mouth at the breast, and she had no particular smell except a vague hint of leaf buds and smoke bombs. Ana María turned her head toward Antonio and looked at him for a long time in a mixture of happiness and impassivity.

From the moment he crossed the threshold, she understood that prison had changed her man. He was wearing a dirty old suit without a shirt, was holding his tie, and had rags stuck under his arm that were soaked with the blood from his forehead. A thick beard, so black it was almost blue, covered his face from the base of his neck to the roots of his eyes, and made him look like a castaway. His gaze, beaten down by humiliations and privations, had acquired a steely coldness. He was thinner, bonier, and appeared much older, and for the first time Ana María recognized in him the signs of the old man he would become. He was squeezing his wet crumpled tie in his fist with the same worried and determined hardness that she read in his eyes, and he let go of it only when Ana María offered him his daughter wrapped in a white blanket.

Antonio took her as if he were holding in his hands one of the twelve stones of Israel. Wriggling there in his arms, she looked like a nymph dancing in an olive pit. The child weighed an immeasurable weight, that of yesterday and that of tomorrow. It was like the discovery of a fresco found after an excavation, an enclosed treasure, a whole world of symbols to be deciphered. Antonio, who had until then maintained a serious tension and reserve in his gestures, fell to his knees and burst into tears.

"What name do you wish to give your child?" the nurse repeated.

He could not find a single word, not for his wife nor for his child, as if the soft torrent of that moment had purged him of all language. Ana María then spoke. In the deafening ruckus coming from the streets, she replied with a firm voice, "She will be called Venezuela."

Venezuela

Of all the children born that day, it was impossible to imagine that Venezuela would not become a free woman. She seemed to have taken on the strength of the revolt that ardent afternoon, when a cry had pierced the city and the streets were aflame with rapture and ruin, as if she had distilled the raucous dignity of a people in the heart of her name. Eager and hungry for everything, she grew up with the energy of a riot. As a little girl, she did not go through that period of erasure and abandonment that her mother, Ana María, had known at the same age, which she had crossed blindly, without grasping what was real, nor the disordered energy of young Antonio when he had stolen a canoe on the shores of Santa Rita, but within her a hunger was rising like a tautly drawn bow, a discipline, a necessity.

To everyone around her it was only natural and indisputable that Venezuela should become a doctor. That destiny was already traced out for her with such prophetic confidence that no one ever doubted it, nor did they consider the weight that a mother's overwhelming talent and the blazing renown of a father might represent for a child. One evening, Ana María gave Venezuela the gold penguin brooch that her own mother, Eva Rosa, had bequeathed to her.

"There are family treasures that are priceless," she said. "I am certain you will go far."

As she said these words, Ana María was thinking that her daughter would go far not only in life but also in the world. She had come to this understanding one day when she happened to find Venezuela playing with a wooden truck that she had rolled through the whole house to the front door, then into the street, then under the cars on the pavement, her head bowed with carefree nonchalance, and Ana María had been obliged to go collect it from under the skirts of the newspaper saleswomen on the square, for it seemed capable of continuing its journey all the way to the Brazilian border. Everything in her was action, movement, departure, everything in her burned with the desire to explore, and this dream, which in others might have been nothing more than a simple ephemeral childhood phase, remained imprinted in Venezuela's spirit as a need to conquer. She amused herself by reading the shapes of imaginary cities in the bark of birch and beech trees, and she could spend hours interpreting the traces of mildew and the cracks in the walls, seeing them as great ships lost in rivers of plaster.

This obsession was so overpowering that one day, when she was around six years old, her mother opened an atlas before her and talked to her about cities built on mountaintops and hanging orchards in Peru, about the ivory of Ethiopia and the dialects of India, about the celestial ceremonies of Nepal and the dances of the

Antilles, the mysteries of Japan and the secret utopias of Libertatia. She spoke to her about citadels carved into the Burmese cliffs and hamlets on the shores of the Danish fjords, about Mediterranean creeks, Chinese temples, Senegalese markets. Leaning over the map with the concentration of a clockmaker, moving her finger along unknowable immensities of green and blue, Ana María pointed to a minuscule dot in the middle of nothing.

"This," she said, "is where we live."

Venezuela looked at the dot with disappointment. She traversed the countries, the oceans encircling them, the coastlines running to the south, and she could not shake a feeling of sadness. If she had discovered a whole cosmography in that little blot that her mother was pointing to, she could not imagine the thousands of others that were yet to be explored, so distant and yet so close. She felt excluded, banished from the thousands of cities where incredible universes were fermenting, whose root systems continued to grow while she, isolated and out of reach of these riches, was wasting time, day after day, feeling less and less in the right place.

Antonio feared that his daughter would want to travel the world too soon. When she turned seven, he made sure to take her out as rarely as possible, in order to give her a taste for patience and the contagious charm of solitude. At that time, in the house on Avenida 3H, his mother-in-law, Eva Rosa, had come to live with them, having finished raising her four children from three different husbands. Venezuela started tenderly calling her Mama Eva.

She was then in her sixties. After a lifetime of washing laundry and kneading bread, she had returned to the Catholic realms of her youth, making crowns for altar decorations and yard-high candles. She no longer had the tropical beauty of her days with Chinco Rodríguez and the penguin brooch. Time had erased her splendid lightness, her passionate heart, but she had kept her incredibly pale skin, without a wrinkle, which she still protected from the sun with a woven straw hat, while she looked at the silent street from her balcony with its metal railings, as she had done years ago in the house of Papa Zoilo.

Attentive and obliging, she had dedicated her life to helping others, always took the wing when chicken was served, and had never contradicted anyone at the table. She was so discreet, so transparent, that one wondered whether she might not disappear altogether someday, for she seemed to be gradually fading, and when Venezuela hugged her, she would stay for a long time in her embrace, as if she wished to hold her grandmother back a little longer and prevent her from slipping away.

This old lady with her perfectly set hair, who smelled of soap and olive oil, and would spend her afternoons filling jugs of tamarind juice and watering the bougainvillea vines in the garden, was visited every Wednesday after her siesta by a neighbor, whose frivolous company gave her the feeling of growing younger. Her name was Zina.

No one knew much about Zina, only that she was the daughter of a family of immigrants from Syria and that in her youth a French film producer, who happened to be passing through Maracaibo and was fascinated by the pulchritude of her eyes, had proposed to take her across the Atlantic and make her a celebrity in Paris.

But her parents had opposed the plan, convinced that this producer was no more than a sweet-talking ruffian. And that is why she remained in Maracaibo without rebelling, contemplating the years flying by, and also why she spent her life compulsively watching all the French films of the 1950s with insatiable nostalgia. These black-and-white films, dubbed in Castilian Spanish with a Madrid accent, brought clarity to the memory of that man who had disappeared into the film reels of the world. As if the love scenes at which she sobbed in silence had been shot solely for her, she saw him in every gentleman on television, and was convinced that he sent her coded messages through these characters, in the dialogues she repeated in front of her mirror, with her mascara dribbling down her cheeks.

For as long as Venezuela could remember, Tía Zina had always been there, sitting in her cotton dress on the porch, shaded by an awning of flowers, observing the world and its ways without anyone ever noticing her existence. Her skin had withered, her breasts were crisscrossed with veins, her heart had folded in on itself like a slow wrinkle. Time passed, and her age became such an approximate number that even she could not remember her birth date with any certainty. People were born and died in the neighboring houses, the governments rose and fell in succession, electricity arrived, automobiles replaced trams pulled by mules, the Virgin of Chiquinquirá was crowned with a diadem made of seventeen pounds of gold and sapphires, Carlos Gardel performed at Teatro Baralt, two wars shook the world, a statue was erected of Queen Wilhelmina, the bridge on the lake was inaugurated, the capital sent the torch that was to celebrate the first Olympic Games from Maracaibo, and in the middle of this disorderly and tangled century, Zina continued on, immobile and untouchable, sitting under her awning, wearing the same cotton dresses, daydreaming about impenetrable things. No man had ever been able to explore the mute realms inhabited by her silence, since she had made the decision, on the day the French producer departed, to marry a man only if he offered to take her across the Atlantic, but that stranger never found the alleyways leading to her heart and he too had gotten lost in the knots of history.

More or less at this same period, she happened to come across an article with a photograph of Claudia Cardinale, perhaps the most beautiful woman of the 1960s, and discovered that she had gone through an incredible transformation. From a scrawny, bony tomboy born in a little apartment in Tunis to the best-paid

Italian actress of her time, she had become within a few years one of the wealthiest and most desirable celebrities in the world, the dream of every man and boy and the envy of every woman and girl on earth, and her phenomenal measurements had left such a profound mark in the annals of beauty that for almost thirty years it was impossible for a fashion model not to be compared to her.

Zina was plunged so deeply into the myth of this woman, who navigated in a nebula of European soirees, that one cloudy morning in December, when she was drinking coffee with Eva Rosa in her garden, she noticed Venezuela playing on the lawn dressed in a light linen skirt and saw this as a sign. She must have been about seven years old. Seeing the alarming thinness of the girl, Zina remembered in a flash the metamorphosis of Claudia Cardinale and foresaw, in the little girl's figure, a splendid future.

From then onward, she came to the house on Avenida 3H every day and got it into her head to subject Venezuela, from the start of the dry season, to a program of physical training of Hollywoodian intensity, in the unshakable conviction that she could offer her the destiny of which she herself had been robbed.

Zina made Venezuela take French and Italian lessons, concocted a diet for her based on chicken and cucumbers, and started believing so ardently in her implausible plan that every time she looked at the girl's skinny little body as she tried to shape it, her face would light up with delight and hope, imagining the future curves and voluptuousness to come, where nature had carved only right angles and parallel lines. For several long months, Zina spoke about this to no one, keeping the secret within the family circle until the day when some children were mocking Venezuela, and she warned them: "You'll see, this girl will be more beautiful than Claudia Cardinale and she will go to Paris."

However, puberty did not make Venezuela's body blossom in the same way as Claudia Cardinale's. She was not well-endowed and quite short, like her mother, and had that openhearted look that protected youngsters often have, while her chest remained similar to a puppy's, and her waist did not present any dizzying curves. She managed with great difficulty to pad out her shape by filling her dresses with nine cotton lawn petticoats festooned with embroidered ruffles and stuffing her brassieres with wads of fabric. She did not develop the Pompeian beauty that had been prophesied for her, but her charm was visible in other ways, in the magnetism of her eyes, in her curly black hair, inherited from her mother, that cascaded down her back in ringlets, while all the natural imperfections in her face did not allow her to pursue a career in the movies.

Zina, who had always maintained an interest in the world of spirits, and was certain of being right, wanted to investigate her future as others investigate the past. Acknowledging the failure of her experiment, she took Venezuela by the arm one evening, crossed Plaza Baralt, walked down Avenida Urdaneta past the Calle

Carabobo, and arrived near Sector Veritas where a clairvoyant with the name of a queen, Catalina Segunda, had them come into her candlelit room. Venezuela was expecting to find a Gypsy with large gold hoop earrings and a tattooed mouth, smelling of camphor and sandalwood, but instead there appeared a young woman of Mediterranean elegance, wearing a white silk dress and a crown made of stags' antlers, with the absent expression of someone who spends more time speaking with the dead than the living. When Venezuela appeared before her, she drew two cards and in a melodious voice, punctuated with intuition and melancholy, uttered these enigmatic words: "You will go only when you have freed yourself of the weight of the gold."

"What gold?" Venezuela asked.

"Yours."

This vague reply brought her no peace, but Zina gave it great credence. She assured Venezuela that the tarot was never wrong, and when she got home, Venezuela got caught up in the game and thought about that gold with such insistence, with such constancy, that she felt as if everything around her had started glistening with an annunciatory glow. She then started forlornly looking for it everywhere around her, in every prediction, in every sign, in every symbol, with the eagerness of a truffle dog. This obsession fascinated her as much as it frightened her, for she was able to measure the inescapable, cruel risks of this quest for gold, which were deeply anchored in the collective memory of her country. She was only rid of it when she learned, during a class about the Spanish conquest, that Lope de Aguirre, who was called Aguirre the Madman after he assassinated thousands of men while searching for the kingdom of El Dorado, had been hacked into ten pieces at his death, each of which had been carried in ten different directions, and that his head had been locked into an iron cage at El Tocuyo and exhibited in the middle of the public square. She only understood Catalina Segunda's words many years later, during a tombola game one afternoon, when she realized which gold the fortune teller had spoken of and decided to let go of the weight of the family myth once and for all.

At that moment an old woman arrived at the house on Avenida 3H. Venezuela was reading in the living room when she felt a presence on the porch and found the woman sitting alone on one of the three front steps, as tattered and sad as a wounded sparrow. She had a few bags of cornmeal heaped in her lap and looked so ill that Venezuela invited her inside and led her through the house into the garden, thinking that she was one of those destitute patients coming for a consultation. The old woman gazed up at the splendor of the ceilings, the brilliance of the mirrors, the expanse of the inner courtyard, and the dozens of diplomas hanging on the walls in a constellation of wax seals. When she was sitting in front of Venezuela, she said not a word, but remained perfectly erect and impassive on her chair with her hands flat on her thighs, examining the candelabras on the shelves. After a moment, she emitted a faint sound: "Tonio?"

Venezuela had her father called, and he arrived in the living room without haste. He stared at the old woman distractedly then with a fleeting expression of love and tenderness so intense that he had to bite his lip so as not to cry. He threw himself into her arms.

"Who is this?" Venezuela asked in astonishment.

"This is my mother," Antonio replied with a trembling voice.

Mute Teresa was given a room at the back of the house that had once been Antonio's office but had been turned into a guest room. It was furnished mainly with bookshelves filled with medical texts in Latin. He led her into it with the distinction reserved for great ladies. She sat down at once on the corner of the bed, her head bowed, taking up as little space as possible, and would not let go of the bags of flour on her lap. Her body was so shriveled that it did not move when she breathed but made a discreet rasping sound and a soft hiss that seemed to come from the depths of the ages.

Before leaving her, squeezing both of her hands, Venezuela assured her that she was most welcome to live with them as long as she needed to. Mute Teresa found it so difficult to reply that no sound came from her mouth. She made a few signs at Antonio.

"What is she saying?" Venezuela asked.

"She is saying she has not come here to live but to die."

Two days later, one June morning, Mute Teresa did not appear at breakfast as she usually did. Antonio waited, but Venezuela felt an ill omen in the air.

"She won't come," she said.

Antonio rushed into the back room and found Teresa lying in a rocking chair in the middle of a ray of sunlight, her arms hanging, her head tipped back, her eyes half closed. He approached her slowly and leaned over her face. It took only a glance to realize she had died during the night, far from those church steps where she had spent her beggar's life, and never had her expression shown such deliverance. In the deep brown of her iris, a fine line of light evoked the infinite words she had not been able to pronounce and that now, in the kingdom of heaven, no longer condemned her to silence.

Antonio kissed her face and her hands. He then knelt at her feet, put his cheek on her inert knees, and started crying softly, mixing his tears with the cornmeal. She was buried in the back courtyard of the house, her body covered in a white shroud. Before her mouth was closed, mango seeds were put on her tongue so they could take root where the body was buried, and Antonio filled the grave with a little cold soil.

The death of Mute Teresa coincided with a period of great prosperity for Antonio. He was active, enterprising, decisive. He paid very little attention to his family, to Ana María who was often absent, or to Venezuela who was already thirteen and being raised by Eva Rosa, for all the energy that he should have devoted to them was absorbed by his work. Before the dream of a university came to overturn his destiny, Antonio performed 1,134 operations, and not a single patient died under his hands. Of the twenty hospitals in Maracaibo, he was the director of six, was the president of the College of Medicine, the founder of the Federation of Medicine of Venezuela, a representative in the national Congress, a survivor of the epidemics of hookworms and malaria, and led the medical team that managed to eradicate smallpox from the area. Every morning his doorstep was littered with envelopes, invitations, and awards. The new governor, Wolfgang Larrazábal, wanted to give him the keys to the city, but Antonio refused the distinction, and even his most virulent detractors recognized in this political gesture a humility that proved his noble character.

Fables and stories were told throughout Maracaibo that fed the legend of Antonio Borjas Romero. Some people said that his father was an Italian monk who had traveled fourth class on an ocean liner heading for Panama, where he intended to live a cloistered life in a lepers' colony, but who had decided to spend one last night with a woman, and that Antonio was born of this night of repentance and devotion. Others were convinced that his father was an English lord, a chamberlain, a powerful man who never had time for anything but did find an hour to get a young mute woman pregnant and had then disappeared in the corridors of the British Parliament, leaving behind only two cigarette rolling machines. What was certain was that Antonio Borjas Romero had become a doctor so well known in the region and a cardiologist so respected that his name resounded in all the towns surrounding Maracaibo, from Guajira to Bobures, with almost a mythological aura.

He was admired in Santa Fe in particular, a little village of drums and wooden saints, where there lived a certain Clemente Pájaro, a legendary ne'er-do-well who had become the richest man of the south of the lake through contraband tobacco trading, and whose progeniture was so numerous that he was called "papa" all the way to the Colombian border. According to the tales told by the sugarcane cutters, the version that was most commonly repeated was that Clemente Pájaro was the son of an old *mantuano* family, descendants of Spaniards, an aristocratic branch of white Europeans born in America, who had grown rich in the sugar trade, and who had built such a large house that ships on the ocean could see its lights in the middle of the night before they saw the beam of the lighthouse.

It was said that his father had been throttled by one of his own servants in a fishermen's whorehouse, and that he was found five months later on the other side of the country, his body trussed up like a plucked rooster. After his death, young Clemente's family fortune had been stolen from him by his diabolical uncles. He lived in abject poverty until the day his uncles died in turn, one from a hernia of the colon and the other stabbed by a young homosexual lover, known as Alanito.

Clemente Pájaro, who was fourteen at the time, burned both corpses in the garden around the family house, of which he became the sole proprietor; sold all the furniture that his family had collected over five generations; replaced all the servants by brigands in his service; and mounted one of the biggest networks of illegal tobacco trafficking from the obscurity of his home, building his fortune on the deaths of all the Pájaros that had come before him.

That was why, when an acute bout of renal colic deprived him of his power of speech and led him to founder in a swamp of black fevers, Clemente Pájaro judged that the only man capable of touching his abdomen was Antonio Borjas Romero.

In the middle of the dry season, he left his kingdom of contraband, traveled along the lakeside for a week, crossed the valleys of the Altagracia in a horsedrawn carriage, and immediately headed for the doctor's office. One afternoon in March, at twenty-four minutes past three, during the siesta, he presented himself at the central hospital of Maracaibo, flanked by four armed men. He entered the building with a pair of six-shooters in his jacket and a heavy two-foot-long machete hanging from a strap. He climbed the stairs to the reception area and said curtly to the young woman at the desk, "I want to see the doctor."

Without even raising her eyes to him, she continued filling out a form.

"The doctor is busy," she replied.

In a calm gesture, Clemente Pájaro got out his machete and laid it down on the form. Then, in a pleasant voice, he repeated, "I want to see the doctor."

The young receptionist sighed and said with annoyance "Wait here," opened a door behind her, and walked toward Antonio, who was reading at his desk.

"A man wishes to see you, doctor."

Antonio turned to her. "Tell him to come back after the siesta."

The young woman shrugged, exhausted. "If you ask me, if you don't see him, he'll cut your head off."

No surprise appeared on Antonio's face. He closed his book slowly, put his white coat back on, and washed his hands with a soap that left a smell of potassium in the room.

"Tell him to come in."

It took only one look for Antonio to know that this man had not slept for a week, and that he had undertaken a long journey. His clothes were covered in the dust of the roads, and under his jacket he carried an arsenal that could have subdued an entire military division. Antonio did not let him speak. He did not allow him to quench his thirst nor to set down his effects, but had him sit on the little operating table without a word. With a sharp and precise gesture, he pulled down his pants, sterilized a syringe of morphine, pinched his buttock, and jabbed him with a quick blow. Clemente Pájaro gave a high-pitched yelp and the guards waiting outside the office rushed in. Antonio handed them a compress with a comma-shaped bloodstain.

"Give him pomegranate juice and make him piss."

Clemente Pájaro was taken away, supported by the shoulders, and disappeared without paying. Antonio forgot all about him until the following week when his secretary held out a package to him as he arrived in his office.

"It's from the bandit," she said. "I hope it's not his stone."

When Antonio opened the envelope, he found the ownership title for a house on the seaside, in a village called La Rosita. A note accompanied this extravagant present: "A stone is worth a pearl."

The house that Clemente Pájaro gave Antonio was indeed a pearl. The family first arrived at La Rosita one morning as a warm breeze was coming in off the ocean, from Bonaire and Aruba, and shaking the masts on the shore. In the distance other masts rose above the jetty and could be seen beyond the seawall, and farther still a majestic hill with a mysterious humped shape plunged down to disappear into the horizon, almost with the profile of a huge sea creature plunging its head into the abyss. This was the entrance to the gulf of Maracaibo. A peaceful line of worm-eaten canoes, where black mold had burst cracks in the benches, stretched over the water. La Rosita seemed to be fixed in a time without time. All that remained of her was her name, which was still present in the memory of a few wealthy families who had come to the area to build holiday homes, which were now abandoned manors. When oil was discovered, the latifundistas and the young bachelors had deserted the coast to go work on the rigs and in the mines. Only a few families of fishermen remained, but they were worn out by epidemics and disasters and started planting yuccas. Some of them had returned. After years in the big city, eaten away by poverty and downtrodden by the hierarchies of men, they had come home at the end of a lost battle, as poor as when they left, to take up their place in the past again.

The house that was shown to Antonio's family stood tall on the beach looking out over the ocean, with the gentle menace of a boat heading upstream, in the center of a piece of land occupied by goats and metallic beetles. Its name was La Enconchada, but the first thing that Ana María did, before she even crossed the threshold, was to rename it by making the sign of the cross three times at the front door.

"It will be named Alegría."

First she had the heaps of old junk that had been rotting in the rooms for years emptied out, the weeds pulled from the cement on the porch, and all the rusted bars at the windows replaced by mango-wood shutters. She ordered the exterior walls to be painted an impossible blue, like the one she had seen in a book, covering the Ishtar Gate twenty-five centuries before her own, so that it blended into the sky, and in the garden, where there was already a circle of wild palm trees, she planted an araguaney tree with yellow flowers. Waging a ferocious battle against nature, she spent three days chasing the golden spiders that populated the eaves and the cavities in the stone facades, and filled the cracks in the plaster where the beige-and-black leopard-skin-patterned geckos had made their nests. Under the pretext that the finest houses were those that had no locks, she had the latches removed from all five doors and forbade them from being shut, so that light could fill the rooms in a torrent, and she installed an oil lamp on the veranda, fully convinced that she would spend the rest of her life reading at night and contemplating the sleeping sea.

The morning after their arrival, Antonio and Venezuela took out a canoe and after a few minutes on the water, arrived on a little deserted island, a solitary rock rising above the waves. It was one of those *cayos* that are scattered along the Venezuelan coast. They were called *cayos* as if the stone were a callus on the skin of the water, for all that was to be found on them was vegetation bleached by salt, dry scrub with its roots planted in the sand, and the nests of migrating birds that the storms blew out to sea.

The *cayos* had always been there, their hunchbacked masses rising above the waves, standing up against the wind like the backs of drowned giants. Men would sometimes land there for a break during long fishing trips, hanging their hammocks in a tangle of wild branches, lighting fires, and in time those stones had taken on the sacred aspect of forgotten places, of distant witnesses of the passage of people and their invisible memories.

"No one comes here," said the boatman. "There's not a tree, not a leaf, not a flower. It's completely bald. That's why it's called Cayo Pelón."

Antonio looked around. All he could see was the rock and the sea.

"The place is perfect," he said. "All it needs is one thing."

"What does it need?" Venezuela asked.

"A hospital."

Antonio got it into his head to build a doctor's office on that rock in the middle of the sea, battered by the sun. They had boxes of medicine and supplies brought over, which he and Venezuela set down on crates, piles of aspirin and penicillin sitting on the bare ground. They set up an examination table in the middle of the cabin, between two rocks swollen with fossils.

Much later, when she was living in Paris, Venezuela would so often think about that little shack in the middle of the sea, where her father put boxes into imaginary drawers, where he gave her his first lessons in medicine in the stiff wind of the shores of the Caribbean, that she felt as if she could stretch out her hand and touch that memory. She had so often revisited in her dreams those moments of closeness and joy when they had raised the wooden structure together, stretched the canvas of the walls, swept the sand from the floor. From a distance it looked like a contraband depot. The only thing that indicated that it was a medical outpost was the white flag with a red cross on the roof, which Venezuela had painted herself along with the name: Hospitalito de La Rosita.

The next morning, while Antonio was slowly waking up from a long night, his daughter rushed into his bedroom.

"Look at the sea!" she shouted.

Antonio took a while to get over his astonishment when he opened the shutters of the living room and saw, floating on the surface of the water, dozens of boats in single file facing the dispensary, a long column of canoes and dinghies lining up at the entrance of the Cayo Pelón.

These were all the inhabitants of La Rosita and the surrounding villages, men and women most of whom had never seen a doctor, workers with wrinkled faces and hands worn by fishing, children with swollen bellies and red eyes, a whole silent population who had rushed there at dawn when the rumor had spread that a doctor was giving consultations on a rock. They had nothing to pay him with, except their generosity. In the bottom of their canoes they brought fresh fish and coconuts picked that morning, cooked corncobs and baskets of hot flatbreads, little captured turtles and gutted iguanas ready to be skewered and cooked on a grill.

Antonio would examine them and give directions to Venezuela who, sitting on a mountain of boxes of medicines, would get out pills of different colors that she would place under their tongues. Since most of the patients could not read, she found a metaphor so they would not get the pills mixed up.

"The sun is red when it comes up in the morning, so: red pill in the morning. The sun is blue when it sets in the evening, so: blue pill in the evening."

On the weekends, Antonio thus became a seaside general practitioner, working for free, wearing shorts and espadrilles, whereas from Monday to Friday he was the cardiologist of the main hospital in Maracaibo, laden with honors and responsibilities, a respected and respectable man, who only treated the city's wealthiest residents. No split pulled at his heart, no incongruity. This contrast allowed him to realize that he was not part of that world nor the other, that one supported the other, that one justified the other.

One morning, an old sailor with his face covered in mud disembarked on the *cayo*, his irises circled by grayish rings. He had light-colored eyes that he was able to open more easily underwater than in the air, which led Antonio to believe that his nascent cataracts were no more than a crust of salt that the sea had deposited between his eyelids like a white sediment on the cornea. No one could say precisely whether it was diving or old age that had made him lose his sight, but until the moment Antonio operated on him, after which he rediscovered the colors of the sunset and the silver scales of porgies, he had become almost blind and could only find his way underwater by the movement of submarine waves.

"I am as blind as Homer," he said.

Antonio did not recognize him at once and thought that he was a poor man corroded by the harshness of his trade. He must have been at least a hundred years old. His skin smelled of seaweed and boats, his white hair fell on his shoulders in thick tresses, and in his weary gaze were traces of the dereliction of the century that his eyes seemed to have followed into its most distant regions. Despite his deliquescent Spanish, he appeared to speak other unknown languages, for the intonations in his voice had the suppleness of Indigenous dialects, and Antonio wondered if he hadn't seen him somewhere before. He asked him for the reason for his visit, all the while trying to search through the abysses of his features for an old acquaintance, but time had covered the tracks on his face.

"Look at what I brought you," the old man said.

He got out a cigarette rolling machine and Antonio understood that this blind sailor, worn down by the world, was none other than Elías.

Still just as garrulous, he launched into never-ending tales of his voyages throughout the Caribbean. He had carried smugglers of silver scorpions from the islands of Barbados to Martinique, but had shipwrecked off the coast of San Domingo when a cage sprang open and half the crew had succumbed to the stings. In the bay of Costa Rica, he had spent a year with a team of treasure-hunting divers who went down into the deep to find the lost coffers of sunken Spanish galleons, but who discovered only copper coins from the Merovingian period with mere historic value, so they threw them back into the water. He said he had protected a minister with his own chest during an official visit when a madman had tried to stab him with a knife. He had profaned the burial sites of Guatemala, slept with caciques' daughters, towed a hundred ceremonial canoes for the majestic funeral of a Nicaraguan general, witnessed the childbed of a queen on an island, found a gold nugget as big as his fist in the belly of a tamandua and lost it in a card game off the coast of Colombia.

Antonio, who owed a debt to this man for having saved him from the Majestic, the day when he gave him the letter for Don Victor Emiro, took him home and invited him to stay for as long as he wished. He showed him to the room where Mute Teresa had spent her last two days. Captain Elías hung up a mosquito net and did not come out from under it until the following Monday.

One morning, under a menacing sun, when Antonio was absent, Venezuela saw a hundred-year-old man cross the living room completely naked to go to the kitchen for a glass of water. When he first saw her, he apologized for having drunk the water without permission, and not for his nudity, and then greeted her with excessive elegance and refinement, bending low to the ground in a delicate bow, holding out his hand to kiss hers, with manners that he had learned in the salons of the Andean upper classes.

"Who are you, señor?" Venezuela asked.

"My name is Elías Borjas Romero," he replied. "I am your grandfather."

But Venezuela did not have the time to become better acquainted with the toothless sailor whose tongue was devoured by fables and who said he was of her blood, for every morning on the Cayo Pelón, in the little shack with the white-and-red flag, she was obliged to attend to each examination with religious attention.

Because it was impossible for Ana María and Antonio to conceive of their daughter being anything other than a doctor, she too started to believe in this ready-made dream. Her parents talked to her about the illnesses gnawing at the world, retraced the history of epidemics, described the fearsome continents of bacteria, told her of people dying of an invisible virus in the middle of countries with fertile lands and of empires devastated by the invasion of a germ smaller than a speck of dust. Venezuela was surprised by the interminable list of microscopic, imperceptible dangers hidden in the furrows of the air, against which her parents waged a war to the death. Ana María, who was more didactic, knew how to make all this come to life through stories and images. Antonio, less talkative, made her follow the treatment of each patient so that she could learn by observation.

One day a man arrived with a harpoon stuck in his thigh and Antonio decreed that he must be operated on right away.

"You will be my assistant," he said to Venezuela. "This will be your baptism."

Venezuela would remember for the rest of her life the violent spasms that wracked the fisherman's body when Antonio pulled the spearhead out of him, the white foam on his lips and the puddles of blood so thick that the sand could not absorb them. She would remember until her death the screams of pain losing themselves on the waves in the distance, the wan look she could read in his eyes. She would never forget the hideous grimace that deformed his mouth, his clenched fists punching into the void, his chest rocking with convulsions. She would cast her mind back with horror, much later, to that barbarous and filthy scene, where that poor man was sliced open and emptied like a fish, and to the way he continued to shake when he was put into a canoe on a stretcher made of braided rushes to be taken home. Venezuela saw him pass in front of her, plunged into motionless torpor, as if he were dead, his leg open like a watermelon, and she felt the need to vomit.

Antonio, who had undertaken this operation as an uneventful morning's work, washed his hands in the sea while reminding his daughter of the importance of hygiene after each operation. He straightened up and looked at the time.

"I'm hungry," he said. "How about you?"

Not only was Venezuela not hungry, but it took her four days to regain her appetite. This scene marked the end both of her childhood and of the prophecy that had been pronounced for her. Upset by the fisherman's cries, which she could still hear resounding in her head, realizing with terror that she lived under the same roof as butchers, she was so shocked by the carnage she had witnessed that she developed a categorical rejection of anything connected in any way with the *hospitalito.* She never set foot again in the shack on the Cayo Pelón with her father and, from that day forward, would not allow any talk of medicine in her presence.

In the solitude of her childhood, Venezuela was attracted more than ever by the lands she had glimpsed in the illuminations of her mother's atlases and had already started developing an improbable strategy to leave Maracaibo, when a brother made a sudden entrance into her life. One Sunday around noon, a desolate woman, her eyes filled with infinite sadness, was brought to the house on Avenida 3H on horseback. She was accompanied by a ten-year-old boy whose face had the delicacy of a jewel. She had asked to be taken to the door of the *doctora*'s house, and once the owner of the horse had dropped her off, he had taken the money, turned around, and gone back to his field. Her name was Elena. She knocked on the door, said she was six months pregnant, but that she felt her baby was not doing well. She had been turned away everywhere.

Venezuela took her to see Ana María at the hospital that same day. After an ultrasound, Ana María told the mother that the fetus had anencephaly and would probably die during delivery. Moreover the mother had a long-standing liver problem and vaginal lupus, and Ana María explained that she was putting her life in danger if she did not have an abortion. The ten-year-old by her side said nothing. To ensure the mother's survival, Ana María decided to conduct the abortion, but the Supreme

Court of Justice of Venezuela learned of this act that was judged abhorrent and warned that it would be punished by law. The government then subjected Elena to all the practices necessary to deliver the baby. A caesarean was conducted to avoid legal problems. The baby was stillborn, and two weeks later Elena was buried in a local cemetery where a priest waved a bronze thurible, which left a smell of burned earth in the air.

The only survivor of this tragedy was her first child, the ten-year-old with the perfect face. All that was known of him were two things, for his mother whispered, just before she went into the operating theater: "His name is Pedro. He doesn't like eggplant."

Since no one came to claim him, and since the orphanages were at capacity, Ana María wanted to put him in the care of the church, who rejected him because of his mother's impurity. That was why Eva Rosa was awakened suddenly that Sunday morning by an insistent knocking at the door. She put on a long dressing gown and rushed into the front hall, thinking that a tragedy had occurred, when she saw Ana María, in the middle of the street, holding a child sobbing on her shoulder and looking at her with an expression of resignation and doom. Eva Rosa was astonished and led them into the garden. As she was closing the door, she had a vision of a cascade of carnations landing on the boy's head, their petals forming a halo of purple in his hair. Contemplating this scene, Eva Rosa had the feeling that this apparition was part of a divine ceremony, but she was unable to understand its meaning. Nevertheless it seemed obvious to her that the child should henceforth bear the name of this flower, called *clavel* in Spanish, such that when she was informed that his name was Pedro, she replied like a promise: "He looks like a little *clavel.* We will call him Pedro Clavel."

Pedro Clavel thus spent his childhood under the care of Eva Rosa, who looked after him as if he had come out of her own womb. This old woman, exhausted and almost deaf, had retained the innocent kindliness that had guided her all her life, convinced of the idea that one only has what one gives. No one in the household was better suited to raise this orphan of God, this pitiful offspring of love and injustice, and she herself was unaware that he would soon be visited by all the spirits of the mountains of Chivacoa and would found a revolutionary movement in the south of the cordillera.

She found words for his fears, remedies for his wounds, and lavished silent predictions on him with religious devotion. Having unwittingly adopted the gestures and intonations of this distinguished elderly lady, Pedro Clavel soon developed manners of refined feminine grace. While Antonio was working at the hospital and Ana María at the maternity clinic, while Venezuela was teaching him to read and write and telling anyone who would listen of the miraculous arrival of her brother, he built an unassailable knowledge of the most cryptic and convoluted arcana of feminine nature, which would later afford him conquests that would be the envy of any man.

After a while, no one could actually remember the circumstances under which he had arrived at the house, and in the thick heat of the afternoons, only the overpowering superiority of habit persisted.

The generosity of this act, which Ana María undertook in a surge of altruism without thinking of the consequences, made the rounds of the city. Everyone had an opinion on this affair, and the story piqued the indiscretion of unwed mothers so much that the rumor soon spread that *doctora* Rodríguez had turned her house into an orphanage.

But what surprised the neighborhood even more was the fact that as Pedro Clavel grew up, he developed, to the general astonishment of the cigarette sellers and the donkeys on the pavement, an almost embarrassing beauty. His fine profile, his full and shapely lips, his perfectly aligned teeth gave him a perpetually feline expression. His small round head was soon covered by intense black locks that provoked many a girl's sleepless night and caused him to be preceded, wherever he went, by a murmur of agitation full of sighs. His slow gestures, his white hands, and his light green eyes, which were quite uncommon in that part of the world, ended up attracting all the compliments of his female neighbors.

"*Cristo hermoso*," they would say as they watched him pass by. "He looks like a movie star."

In the middle of adolescence, at an age where all the boys were pimpled and lanky, he grew to be a head taller than the others, acquired a square jaw that gave him the air of a Macedonian warrior, and let his hair grow into magnificent thick silky curls, which made him, at fourteen, the handsomest boy that Maracaibo had ever seen. The stunning brilliance of his face was so perfect that no one, not even his own sister Venezuela, knew what to do with this angelic being that seemed to have been born not from an ordinary woman but from waving prairies of purple clover, reddened by the blood of a god, such that everyone started saying that he had arrived at Lake Maracaibo as the penguin once had in Sinamaica, in other words sent by higher powers on the roads of the great north.

And so, when Zina, the neighbor, came into the back courtyard one spring morning and saw him picking mangoes shirtless, the vision of this orphan revived an obsession that she had forgotten since the failure of her physical training of Venezuela and since the French producer had passed through Maracaibo almost half a century ago, and she was convinced that this boy had no place there. Once more she was incapable of thinking of anything else. Consumed by this fixed idea, she was certain that Pedro Clavel was promised to a great destiny, for a Gypsy who read cards had predicted this through vague allusions, and from that day forward, she got it into her head that he must go to the old continent at any price to become an actor.

"There are only savages here," she said to Eva Rosa. "France is the only country that will appreciate his beauty at its rightful value."

She rallied all the neighborhood women, who procured foreign fashion magazines published twenty years previously, where Hollywood actors who were already dead posed in black tuxedos. They dressed him in a wedding suit borrowed from the baker Julito Toronto, perfumed him until there was nothing left of his natural smell, and headed out all together, holding Pedro Clavel by the arm, dressed in their Sunday best and as excited as schoolgirls, to the photographer on Plaza Baralt to have his portrait taken and sent to Paris.

It was impossible not to hear about this event. As soon as they passed in front of a house, the residents would come out onto their porches to applaud this wondrous procession where a teenage boy was being paraded like a Phoenician relic, and the old people in the neighborhood, attracted by the tumult in the street, hastily pulled up the blinds of their bedroom windows, and with eyes full of curiosity and promise, were convinced that they were witnessing a scene that would tomorrow be engraved in the glorious annals of European cinema.

Once the photographs were taken, every single inhabitant of the neighborhood went through the Borjas Romeros' living room to proffer their comments on the best head shots that humankind had ever known. A calligrapher from Calle Mérida, a certain Enrique Desarbres, an elegant man from Picardy who had settled in Venezuela and in his youth had written and published a novel entitled *El Paladar* and was thus the only person in the neighborhood to have his name printed on a book, was asked to write the name Pedro Borjas Romero, also known by his stage name Pedro Clavel, on the back of his photographs in penmanship so exquisite that some people thought it was written in French.

All the pictures were slipped into a white envelope, nestled between protective sheets of cardboard. It was a giant procession of old ladies in floral dresses and hair curlers that headed toward the post office in a tight phalanx, after contributing to a kitty, and who dispatched a parcel to the French Cinema, Paris, France, from all the women of Maracaibo, state of Zulia, Venezuela.

The response from Paris was not swift in coming, but no one despaired. There could be no possible doubt that it was only a matter of time and that the moment the photographs arrived at their destination, it would become obvious to all the producers of Saint-Germain-des-Prés that a new Adonis would soon grace the French art of masculine beauty. Days went by, each longer than the last. The wait dragged out, stretched thin, frayed, then the women grew tired of running to the end of the street as a group as soon as the postman appeared carrying a pouch full of letters that were not addressed to them. They grew tired of imagining that every fair-haired sailor who disembarked at the port and lost himself in the stifling maze of alleyways in the old town was perhaps a mysterious messenger from the French cinema, such that, three months after sending the photographs, the hope of receiving an answer was lost and no one ever spoke of Pedro Clavel again.

Only Zina, who refused to recognize this public defeat, perhaps also feeling somehow responsible for this furor that had borne no results, suggested that the letter had got lost in the intricacies of the international postal system and that they had to take new photographs. But she was not able to convince Pedro Clavel. One September afternoon, when she was once again rallying her neighbors to contribute to another kitty, Pedro Clavel locked himself in his room, walled in a silence that made him all the more handsome, after saying these last words of uncommon wisdom: "Let's forget about those photographs. You can't push a river."

Shocked and saddened, Zina wanted to take him to have his future read in seashells to prove to him that she was right. At around this period, in the El Saladillo district, lived Babel Bracamonte, the same shadowy Indian who had made Captain Elías drink tapir blood, an impenetrable man gifted with unsettling magnetism, who knew how to foretell the future in cowrie shells. Pedro Clavel first refused, but Zina insisted so much that he let her lead him to a dark little house with closed shutters, where a tall Black man with his chest decorated with pearls was standing at the back of a room, his eyes filled with incandescent light and his ankles encircled with bracelets embroidered with little bells that made a sibylline noise.

As soon as Pedro Clavel sat down, the man handed him a pair of scissors and asked him to cut a lock of his hair. And while whispering incantations in Yoruba, he set the lock on fire, threw twelve shells on a square hammock on the floor, and leaned over the cowries to read the message they gave.

“I see a journey,” he said in a cavernous voice.

“Where to? To Paris?” Zina hastened to ask, having stayed in the room.

Babel Bracamonte looked into the ashes for a long time. Then he lit a black cigar and started frenetically puffing at it. The tobacco smelled of the sweat of men who worked the land, of the tires lashed to the prows of ships knocking against the quays, of the cannons of the San Felipe castle, of the heads of the stone giants in the depths of the forests, of the skin of sows in the sunshine.

“You will set out in search of yourself,” he said.

“Is that in Paris?” Zina asked again.

But Babel Bracamonte did not reply, for he had just been pierced by a current that threw him to the ground. Pedro Clavel was surprised by this brutal gesture. His eyes rolling into their sockets, his blood burning, his face disfigured by the devil, Babel Bracamonte started moving around the room, shaken by ungainly spasms, violently arching backward, banging his head against the walls, his mouth foaming with animal screeches, his whole body lanced by a spirit. There he was, under Pedro Clavel’s and Zina’s horrified eyes, with all his fever and fury, bounding around like a young bull, cigar in hand, dancing to an unknown music that only he could hear in his head, and that seemed to be the only truth he could fathom.

His lips covered in saliva stained brown by the tobacco, his eyes shipwrecked, capsizing into a world of madness, he could not calm his convulsive shaking, and an ignominious wind filled the room with a stench of decomposing carrion. He was so possessed that the flames of the candles seemed to grow, as if blown up from the inside by a powerful force. Zina was growing pale, her arms in a cross, paralyzed by the spectacle, but it was when he undressed and started writhing along the floor like a flaming snake, revealing his penis that had grown to extravagant proportions, that Zina crossed herself, grabbed Pedro Clavel by the arm, and pulled him outside.

When Pedro Clavel got home, he heard the same music in his head. He paid no attention to that distant sound, but the revelation seen in the shells pushed him further inside himself, into profound solitude. That evening, he could not shut his eyes for the image of Babel Bracamonte turned in his mind like a fly in a closed bottle. He had found him repugnant, sickening, but could not rid himself of his presence. And yet, in the spiderweb of his loneliness, the captivating image of this man covered in pearls, smelling of smoke and cowrie shells, left him with an aftertaste of fascination. He had already guessed that this insane shaman, who boasted of reading in the swamps of miracles, marked a separation between his own protected, tidy, healthy world and another dark kingdom, that of nomadic saints, which secretly attracted him. Later on, he would come to the conclusion that this was not simply awkward curiosity but a quest mixed with sadness.

For several days he hardly left his hammock to eat and drink. He no longer slept. Venezuela was the first to notice the mysterious torment into which his encounter with black magic had plunged him, for she knew her brother's taciturn character and inhibited nature, and the depth of his distress made her fear the worst. After a week, one April night, despite his sister's vigilance, Pedro Clavel slipped into an altered state.

It started around midnight. He heard an ancestral chant rise in his sleep, as his mouth grew dry and his head opened up into an abyss. Something possessed him completely, as if a whole world of ghosts and demons had entered his body. He could not have said at which precise moment he felt that he was losing his life through his skin, and as he fell from the bed, convulsions shook him and an electric charge ran down his back. The chant continued in his head with stabbing intensity, and he believed he could perceive in this ancient lamentation the secret of death. He was not able to grasp its message, his body temperature rose, he was engulfed in delirium, and the fever invaded his imagination until, in the middle of the night, a strident cry screeched inside him.

He felt like he was drowning in a flow of lava, forgot himself in his mystical dream, endured the total obscurity of his mind for a few hours, and recovered it only later, in the middle of the night, at the front door of Babel Bracamonte, who was sitting in the middle of a circle of young shamans disemboweling a dove, his bare chest covered with a white powder. He expressed no surprise when he saw Pedro alone on his doorstep.

"Come in," he said.

Pedro Clavel entered. He could never really remember how he got there, nor how he had found the sorcerer's house, but when he took his place in the circle, he had the feeling of being in the place where his life had been waiting for him. Someone passed him a long olive-wood pipe from which black smoke was rising. Pedro Clavel smoked it without asking any questions.

"Tomorrow will be the decisive day of departure," Babel Bracamonte was murmuring. "You are now ready to go."

The young shamans had their eyes closed. The darkness of the night descended on them and haunted the house. They were about to set out on a long journey. Pedro Clavel left behind him the photographs and the imaginary cities of the producers of French cinema, forgot the nostalgic follies of Tía Zina and the house of the Borjas Romero family, and in a sublime dream met a baby that looked like an eagle, enclosed in a shoebox in the middle of a sugarcane field, floating on a fire that had no end.

What terrified him the most about this ephemeral vision was to feel it as foreboding, as a scene yet to be experienced in an imminent future. He knew he would never be able to rid himself of it except by abandoning himself to it completely. This was on a Friday. The next day, Pedro Clavel did not return home. At five in the morning, he shaved his head. He strung the Shango beads around his neck and left with the sorcerers.

Venezuela discovered his absence only two days later when she opened the door to his room around 10:00 a.m. Nothing remained on her brother's bed but a mess of seashells and dove feathers. She searched for him everywhere, called the police, roused the neighborhood, but not a trace could be found of the departure of Pedro Clavel, to the point where some of the old ladies of the neighborhood, who had never been able to shake off the memory of his beauty, started saying, "That's because that angel had no place here below."

After turning the house upside down, feverishly searching for a clue to explain his disappearance, the only things that attracted Venezuela's attention were the last photographs for the French cinema that she found in his desk drawers. From then on, she was certain in her heart that, one way or another, the family pressure for him to become famous had caused him to run away. This intuition was so tormenting, so clear to her, that from that day forward she never set foot in the cinema of the Teatro Baralt again, and regarded actors, whether on stage or on film, only with taciturn hostility.

Pedro Clavel blindly threw himself into a world of sorcery and possession, of *santeros* and *curanderos*. His body became a receptacle to welcome the spirits of all the altars from La Magdalena to Guiana and ended up sending his followers into an uncontrollable frenzy. In Coro, during an orange sunset, in a mountainous area infested with mosquitoes, he received the warrior Negro Primero, who entered his body with demented vigor, then made him bound from the floor where he was lying and growl words in a language that nobody had ever heard. When he arrived at Yaracuy, during a spirit vigil, he was filled with Gregorio Hernández, the doctor to the poor, as he was entering some caves accompanied by a rope team of Black men in sandals with rotten teeth, and he awoke naked in a pool of vomit, his body covered in welts from a whip, the palm of his hand burned by four cigars he had stubbed out in it one after the other. At Ocumare, in the first light of dawn, Simón Bolívar endowed him with herculean strength, such that it took eight fishermen to bring him down to the ground. At Cata, on the beach, he once fought a bull. Near Cuyagua, on a rum plantation, he was said to have lifted up a cow.

Seen like that, there was nothing left in Pedro Clavel of the sublime young man with alabaster skin and delicate features, the one who was once dragged to Plaza Baralt to have his photograph taken, for now he looked like a fierce Cossack, his closed face was rough and savage, and he was always preceded by a smell of wild grasses and tobacco roots.

While Venezuela was pursuing her studies, Pedro Clavel was discovering the infernal humidity of the forests of Santa Inés, the valleys of Duaca filled with giant trees, the muddy banks of Valencia where Alonso Díaz Moreno had once founded his first city. Later, on his return, he would talk to Venezuela about her country and what her name meant, about the kapok trees covered in spiny bark that burst through the pavement and grew in the middle of streets, about the hillsides of San Juan de Los Morros, guarded by lanner falcons as big as dragons, and about the forests of San Esteban where he had stolen a stone from Campanero, a petroglyph with Indigenous inscriptions representing bulls and reptiles, which would later be pilfered by a dandy thief by the name of Rutilio Guerra.

Pedro Clavel traveled for a long time, freighted with heavy shamanic burdens and the weight of his servitude, until he could no longer feel the muscles in his shoulders or the heaviness of his soul. He journeyed through the country just as much as the country journeyed through him. He was taught how to speak the language of the rain, to recognize the trees that produced milk. On the side of a path, he met the last man in the area, a seller of ceramic trinkets who offered him a shard of pottery where words in a mysterious alphabet told of an ancient vote cast that had condemned a man into exile.

After a week of wandering, he had reached a plain that was so arid that the rocks sweated drops of salt water. It was a plateau where a village of master rum-makers had been built, surrounded by sugarcane fields, and where it was said Henry Morgan and his crew had once been stranded.

Pedro Clavel learned the story of this pirate who had amassed a treasure so vast that it took two frigates with thirty-six cannons to transport it onto dry land. After a shipwreck on the canopy, he had struck out on foot into a laurel and rubber-tree forest, accompanied by a mixed-race slave who carried an oak coffer on his back, shut with twelve silver nails and a silver lock. On the fourth day, Henry Morgan had ordered a hole to be dug and for the coffer to be lowered into it thanks to the ship's ropes. He had then killed the slave, thrown his corpse into the pit, in order to be the only one to know the exact location of the booty, and sworn to come back to collect it one day.

But a few months later, London had signed the order to bring pirates to justice and he had been obliged to flee from port to port, to Barbados, Martinique, and Maracaibo. He had been thrown in prison in England, then pardoned, ennobled, and appointed governor-general of Jamaica. And thus his political duties, the old temptations of buccaneering, alcoholism, and edema had consumed his existence so completely that he never came back and the treasure had remained buried where it was, ten feet deep between mounds of humus and the corpse of a slave, preserved in the myths that can still be found in the black sugar of the Caribbean.

In that village, next to a distillery farm backing onto a hacienda, he made the acquaintance of Diana del Alba, a skinny brunette, very discreet and introverted, with an open face and honey-colored eyes, which she lowered whenever anyone spoke to her.

Her amber complexion attracted him immediately. Pedro Clavel, sure of his powers, did not need to woo her, for the overwhelming beauty of his face, lit by the flames in the fireplaces and the trembling glow of the oil lamps, that irresistible aura he had retained despite his journey to the depths of black magic, stirred in Diana del Alba's heart the most fantastic dreams. They made love in secret, like two fugitives, entwining themselves in cellars full of rumbling barrels, where the stories of specters and ghosts still haunted the breath of folktales, and he was forced to admit that this timid girl, who seemed to be afraid of everything, nevertheless possessed Babylonian erudition and skill in matters of intimacy.

When Diana del Alba noticed she was late in her cycle, had unusual bouts of nausea, and saw her belly gradually swell, she knew that she would not be able to keep this child conceived in secret. That very day, she went to her mother and told her everything. Her mother remained unperturbed, like an ebony statue, said not a word of reproach nor of judgment, but was filled with mute rage at that raping shaman and regretted the loss of the Amazonian tradition by which all men were castrated as soon as they entered women's territory.

Swallowing her shame, she kept calm and said, "Let's see about it tomorrow." The next day, she took her daughter by the arm and led her to La Victoria, a village a few miles away to the south, where her sister lived. She left her pregnant daughter in the care of that old aunt, in a place no one would come looking for her, and returned home. One morning two days later, when Pedro Clavel expressed concern at not seeing her, she replied, "I took her to my sister's. She needed a breath of fresh air."

For nine months, her mother refused to visit her and stifled the village rumors by repeating that her daughter was simply exhausted. No one asked any more questions, and the pregnancy proceeded without any trouble. When the due date arrived, the mother once again made her way to La Victoria and was alone in attending the birth.

She pulled out of her daughter's body a five-and-a-half-pound baby, who was born with her eyes open, and whose color was similar to the wood of oak barrels. All wrinkled and curled up, she was covered in blackish oil, as if all the spirits and all the tobacco of her father had been deposited on her skin. Diana del Alba was so astounded that she was still rocking in her bed when her mother took the baby from her arms.

"It's a girl," she said. "But I forbid you to name her."

Without even taking the trouble of washing her, while the newborn was still screaming, searching for an imaginary breast in the air, she put the baby into a shoebox and left the house. She headed with a determined step to a sugarcane plantation, pushed her way through the sharp leaves, and deposited the box in the middle of the field.

"It's nothing against you, little one. Life is complicated."

It was the season of burn-offs. The next day, the field was set alight to facilitate the harvest, get rid of weeds, and dislodge the snakes. No one heard the cries of the baby who was still alive in the shoebox in the middle of the stalks. Only a dog called Oro, which had come with a gold prospector who answered to the name of El Andalu, started barking at the flames as if feeling the presence of someone in danger.

The dog rushed into the fire and reappeared, smoking all over, with the box between its jaws. To general surprise, a coffee-colored baby was found inside the box. And this daughter of a secret, this girl who had survived an assassination attempt the previous day, and who kept a burn mark on her temple as a scar of her malediction until the end of her life, was miraculously born a second time on that land of battles and rum, without Pedro Clavel ever knowing of her existence. She was named Eva Fuego.

At the very moment when Pedro Clavel was leaving the rum plantation, a war had broken out on the other side of the world, seven thousand miles away, on the Sinai Peninsula. This conflict, which had nothing to do with Venezuela, provoked an oil embargo in the world's wealthy countries and led to a vertiginous rise in the barrel prices in the Caribbean. In less than a year, "Little Venice" became "Saudi Venezuela."

In Maracaibo, the first signs of this prodigious, treacherous period appeared as intense urbanization. Out of the void, Avenida Padilla, Avenida Libertador, Autopista 1, Paseo Ciencias, and the baseball stadium sprang up in the space of a few weeks, so that when people went out into the street, they thought they had been moved during the night to another city. Very soon, families who had never crossed the border started traveling with their private chauffeurs and their housekeepers, their nannies and their creole cooks, in cruise ships where they dined by candlelight while listening to recitals on grand pianos, then they returned home, their arms laden with new suitcases, to concentrate on that patch of land where overconsumption had become law.

This growth was so paradoxical that, from one day to the next, an employee could buy a car with three months' salary, and at the same time the city was widening its sidewalks for the installation of streetlights. While the Cubans arrived in their iron ships from Mariel, while the Salvadorians were fleeing civil war, while the Colombians were pursued by the FARC, while the Nicaraguans were subjected to the Somoza dynasty, thirty thousand Venezuelans already owned holiday homes in Miami and had only one thing to say: "That's not expensive, give me two of them."

The rumor of this phenomenal rise, of its contracts and legendary hospitality, crossed the borders and attracted some of the most ferocious investors. Soon foreign currencies arrived to join the battle in the glorious arena of the markets, as they once did in the kingdom of Lydia, and bolívares minted with the emblem of Simón Bolívar were strewn through all the coffers of the Americas.

On the old port where his statue had been set down so many years ago, there was an influx of industrialists, entrepreneurs, bankers, engineers, and even movie stars, who drove around in cars that were like palaces on wheels, with silver-plated interiors, windows tinted royal blue, and seats padded with swan down. At the tables of sidewalk cafés, voluble and exuberant lawyers would argue and gesticulate, mentioning sums of money that were still unthinkable in the city, and there also were young European architects who had been handed blank checks to build Mesopotamian edifices on the shores of a lake where fishermen still pulled in their nets by hand. Everyone had to get used to this new economy. Seeds and harvests were now subject to free competition, with no threshold or ceiling, and peasants could impoverish or enrich themselves according to the new laws of the market, including those who still dug their furrows using the power of oxen. The Indigenous people of the sierra were forced to jump on this moving train. They started drinking carbonated soda because mass distribution made it less expensive than bottles of water. Everything was imported— guavas, rice, coffee, corn, sugar, everything that this rich land was capable of producing itself—with such devouring and arrogant madness that one would think that the state of Zulia had suddenly become the center of the world.

The residents of Maracaibo did not have the opportunity to slow down this barbarian invasion, any more than they were able to do so when oil was first discovered. The moment they started to complain about how difficult it was to find housing in their own city, already Italians had opened trattorias in the Neapolitan fashion on the main avenues, the Colombians had set up the first discos, the Chinese had taken over the market of liquor stores, and the streets had been transformed into a giant shopping center of luxury products, beauty shops, and delicatessens, all crowded with families of nouveaux riches putting on aristocratic airs.

In the Club Alianza, the New York Philharmonic gave a historic concert. On the jetty, the largest jackhammer in the world was unloaded. In the city center, glass skyscrapers shot up where there used to be houses made from the drystone of El Saladillo, but also the best French restaurants in the region appeared, where French visitors were able to confirm that the mixed-race waiters, although they did not follow all the Parisian rituals, were just as condescending as those in Saint-Germain-des-Prés. Venezuela became the world's top consumer of Scottish whiskey, and in the space of five years, twenty thousand miles of roads were built.

It was such an abrupt and invasive assault that during the first few months there was hardly any Spanish spoken in the bars and if anyone left Maracaibo for two weeks, the city would be unrecognizable on their return, for new buildings were sprouting up like mushrooms and tall, imposing shopping malls had replaced the alleys lined with mango trees that were planted during the dictatorship of Pérez Jiménez.

Only one person was not upset by all this agitation. Venezuela was then a sensible and intelligent young woman. Indifferent to the mayhem shaking the country, she felt no vocation as clear as the one that had guided her parents in their youth, but she was certain that her destiny would be worthy of theirs, without her necessarily following their example. From the day she was born, to that sinister morning when her father had cut open a fisherman's leg, she had endured the burden of their will, bowing to the image they had of her future. This insistence had achieved the contrary effect, and in the solitude of the now almost empty house,

Venezuela lived according to her own choices. Antonio, too busy with managing the hospital, only came home to change clothes and sleep, walking through the rooms like a ghost, unaware of everything taking place there, not suspecting in the least that his daughter was also building a temple in silence. Ana María, for her part, spent all her time working at the maternity clinic and making presentations at other girls' schools. Since Eva Rosa was relegated to the depths of unfathomable old age, putting together flower crowns for her altars and candles for the dead, Venezuela moved around the house as if she lived there alone. She was therefore at liberty to cover the walls with postcards of Paris and posters of the Eiffel Tower seen from all possible angles. Her passion for France transformed the house on Avenida 3H into a Parisian souvenir shop, and she might have forced everyone to speak French if a phantom from the past had not come knocking on the door one morning.

At the end of March, in the middle of a heat wave, a man came into the garden. Venezuela found him there at eleven in the morning, almost hidden by the wide monstera leaves, between the tubs of bougainvillea vines and the violet constellations of carnations, she discovered a magnificent dark-haired man, much taller than she was, with square shoulders and an irresistible gaze. He was smiling at her with surprising familiarity. Despite his voice and the way he moved his hands, it took her a few minutes to realize that this man with empty eyes, tanned skin, and his hair cut short was no other than her brother, Pedro Clavel, who had survived the venom of the yellow toads of the Guianan plateau and the lures of the spirit world.

"Pedro," she said as she embraced him. "You've come back."

No one, not even Venezuela, knew much about him. He was taller than when he left, with a more distracted air, an evaporated attitude, an anchoritic ennui, and something of a morose glow in his eyes that made him seem slightly evanescent. Rumors had been circulating about him. Tired of battling his demons, after a life of shamanism and black feasts, he had seen the misery of the countryside and abandoned villages, and had decided to fight men instead. He had founded resistance movements in the mountains with the Colombians, had gone down past the equator recruiting activists in the unions, had crossed Peru on an unreal journey, then in Chile had enlisted in a far-left revolutionary movement, the MIR, all with the same fervor he had displayed when he left with the sorcerers. Pinochet's coup found him near Santiago, where he was hiding weapons in a vineyard, and he was arrested, tortured, imprisoned, and then released. After traveling through countless cities for five years, he was said to have more than sixty pseudonyms, like Lenin, so that he could not even remember his own name, and after his death the number of his identities had grown to the extent that people continued to call him by different names in three countries.

"What have you been up to all this time?" Venezuela asked.

Pedro Clavel smiled. He still held on to the memory of those devouring climes and the black river of revolt.

"I could try to tell you about my journey, but it would be like trying to describe the ocean by saying that it was simply salt water."

Venezuela was about to ask him how long he intended to stay, but Pedro Clavel was one step ahead of her.

"I won't stay, I need to go."

"Go where?"

"To Europe," he replied. "Maybe Paris."

Venezuela fell silent. Paris, that city as round as a tearstain, crossed by a wrinkle of water, whose silhouette she had been able to see in her mother's atlas, continued to haunt her. That was where she would grow old.

Pedro Clavel left the next morning without a sound, just as he had returned, and the only clue that showed he had in fact slept in the house on Avenida 3H was the hammock he left hanging in his room, like a vestige of a past life. Despite the brevity of his appearance, he left a deep mark in his sister's solitude. Her imagination, nourished only by Zina's fables about Paris and distant rumors, tormented her to the point that she could no longer stand the idea of spending a minute more in Maracaibo, and she could only slake the boredom aroused in her by that city of fake riches and saints' parades, with its haste in catching up its delay in its ridiculous race for glory, when she made a decision that she never changed until her death. Like her brother, she needed to leave.

She would never forget that afternoon when she went into her mother's room, and without letting anything show, sat before her with a sentence burning on her lips. She knew that Ana María would refuse to let her leave Maracaibo. She knew that in that immobile house, where sedentariness had become law, there was no place for nomadic ambitions. The carnations in the garden, the white hammock, the hundred mirrors in the bedroom, the portrait of Chinco on the wall, the serving ladle, the green jug shaped like a fish, the thousand things in her house—all of that would not allow her to leave. And yet, sitting in a rocking chair, looking around at the thousands of old things, with the heady odor of the past filling her nostrils, Venezuela imagined with almost perverse pleasure the upheaval that her decision would cause, and this idea made her smile. Her mother noticed it.

"Why are you smiling?" she asked.

Venezuela did not want to pretend anymore. "Because I want to leave for Paris," she said. "And I am still in this room."

Ana María stiffened in surprise. She looked at her daughter with an expression of dismay and panic, and she could not help thinking of Pedro Clavel, whose abrupt disappearance had left a mark on her like a scar.

"I've already lost a son," she said. "I won't lose my daughter."

Venezuela stayed sitting there, not moving, not speaking, her eyes fixed on her mother's. Ana María added, "Talk about it with your father."

But Antonio was never at home. Venezuela had to make an appointment, as if she had been one of his patients, to be granted half an hour alone with him. He received her at his huge desk, at the center of an air-conditioned room, which he had decorated with furniture brought from France, a sculpture representing two snakes wound around a laurel branch, and a bas-relief of Socrates raising his goblet of hemlock in front of his disciples. He was wearing a white coat over a suit and tie, with a leontine watch chain attached to his collar by a brooch, and anyone who saw him might think this man had never done anything besides manage this institution, that he knew nothing of poverty, and that his poised demeanor and thoughtful air were created only for the rigid climate of hospitals.

Venezuela spoke with a clear, confident voice, as if she were speaking to the doctor rather than to her father.

"I want to go to Paris."

"You will go nowhere. Your destiny is here, with us, in Maracaibo."

This response filled Venezuela with icy rage. She did not understand how parents could teach their children to speak and then not listen to what they had to say. But of all the people in the house, Eva Rosa was the most shocked when she noticed that Venezuela had not come home that night, nor the following one, and she feared that she might have been contaminated by the spirit sickness of Pedro Clavel and only come back years later with her head filled with shamanic rites. In fact, Venezuela had gone to seek refuge only a few yards away, in Zina's house next door. The old Syrian lady, who had learned to decipher Venezuela's silences since the days when she was in charge of her physical training, was the only one to understand the bleeding tear in her heart.

"Parents are sometimes wrong too," she told her. "I'll have a word with them."

Antonio and Ana María would not hear of it. For a while, Venezuela continued to waver between resignation and doubt. Shipwrecked on the shores of sadness, voyaging through her fears, she had almost forgotten the reason for her distress, and had resigned herself to staying in Maracaibo for the rest of her life, to going to medical school and operating on drunk sailors on the *cayos* of La Rosita, when a trivial event one April morning gave her an idea that would change the course of her life.

It was during a charity fundraiser at the Santa Sofia school. In the main courtyard, at around 10:00 a.m., Venezuela had bought a raffle ticket, and her number had won an embroidered white lace mantilla and thirty bolívares to spend in a religious supplies store.

This idea inspired her to organize a raffle herself, of which the prize would be her freedom. Despite the natural authority imposed by her parents, she needed to do something to prove that she was the daughter of two obstinate people. The following week, she elegantly set the gold penguin brooch in a little mother-of-pearl box and organized a lottery for this jewel that her ancestors had passed down from one generation to the next, from the day when the fisherman Martín Gámez had found a penguin on the beach of Caimare Chico.

She sold the raffle tickets in her high-school corridors, presenting her brooch as if it were a crown jewel, giving details of its alloy of precious metals, of vermeil and emeralds, bringing it out of her bag with Florentine precautions, as if she were showing off the weapon used in a conspiracy. The students examined this sparkling object with surprise, this strange beast that had been immortalized with a ruby eye. Venezuela put so much insistence and tenacity in convincing them to participate, begged them with so much zeal, deployed such a storyteller's imagination that, little by little, she managed within two weeks to collect a fortune that would have allowed her to circumnavigate the globe.

On Ash Wednesday, she gathered in the school courtyard all those who had bought a ticket, and had someone pull the winning number at random out of a jar. The day was foggy. When she announced the winner, he raised his hands in the small crowd and approached her to timid applause. His name was Bertrán Levrero Parra. His parents had arrived with the immigrants of the oil bubble, and he intended to make his way in life as a chess player in the Caribbean tournaments. He was a short plump boy, built like an oak barrel, with a round face, chubby hands, and eyes that sparkled with kindness, giving him the appearance of a hostler. He hardly looked at the brooch when Venezuela handed it to him with a mixture of nonchalance and heartbreak, and asked her in a little flutelike voice, "May I invite you to lunch?"

Many years later, when Venezuela learned that Bertrán Levrero Parra, who had become a famous chess player, had bought all the raffle tickets himself in the hope of inviting her to lunch, it was already too late to accord this man the courage and merit that he deserved. At that moment, in the school courtyard, she was still ignorant of the games of love, for the only thought that inhabited her was the relief at that small fortune that she had managed to amass. She suddenly felt free in her choices, sovereign over her own life, and she understood for the first time what the clairvoyant had told her in riddles that evening when Zina had taken her to confront the cards of her future.

To leave, she had to free herself of the weight of the gold, and that gold was the penguin. In her rebirth, holding the money in her fist as if it were Saint Peter's keys, she made a second appointment with her father in his office. Antonio, who had not shifted from his position and knew nothing of the raffle, could not restrain a gasp of surprise when his daughter set down an envelope full of banknotes on his desk.

"I want to go to Paris," she declared resolutely. "And this time you won't be able to stop me."

Antonio shut the book he was reading. He then realized, at that precise moment, with a certain pride that he never admitted to himself, that Venezuela was the only woman in his life to have stood up to him, and for the first time since that long-gone day when he had taken her into his arms when he came out of prison, he was overcome by profound affection.

She had very black eyes with a subtle spark of intelligence, fine regular bangs on her forehead, and a long nose that provoked in men a mixture of yearning and renunciation. He compared her to the image of her mother at the same age, still intact in his memory after so many years, but he could find no trace of resemblance. He became aware with some sorrow that he had slowly lost touch with his daughter without noticing it, that he had not seen her grow up, distracted as he was by his work, and he realized that this distance between them, full of silence and incomprehension, aroused in him a profound regret that it was by now impossible to do anything about. He wanted to hold her back, in a last paternal effort, but did not feel it was legitimate for him to do so. He was disarmed. The great surgeon did not know how to respond. The hundreds of speeches he had given in the most prestigious gatherings, the countless victories over death that he had won in the operating room, the long list of obstacles he had overcome, all this disappeared before this courageous girl with fire in her eyes, whose legacy came from a lineage of persistence.

Antonio rapidly understood that he would be the loser in this duel and so displayed no resistance. He decided to capitulate for good only when he had her sit down in front of him and uttered these words that would remain in her memory all her life.

"Okay. You can go. But remember one thing: We are slaves to what we say and masters of what we keep to ourselves."

Venezuela set her departure for the end of the rainy season. Between the moment when the penguin brooch was sold and the day Venezuela left the family home, Eva Rosa barely had time to fill her suitcases with dresses embroidered with her name, with forty-seven spare outfits and the seventy-three posters of Paris she had once stuck to the mirrors around the house, along with hundreds of other forlorn trifles from a glorious past that had delayed her exile for twenty years. But Venezuela refused to keep for her rebirth what she had rejected during her entire youth. And so, during the following days, she busied herself with making what remained of her in Maracaibo disappear. She emptied her room, not wanting to leave anything in the drawers of memory, gave away her books, and during a morning spent in a canoe, heading out to deep water with a boatman, threw the last of her worldly goods into the lake with the same solemnity as her great-grandfather Papa Zoilo, on the day when he got rid of his sixteenth-century weapon. All she kept was the raffle ticket that allowed her this liberty.

Antonio did not want to talk about it anymore. He understood that his daughter's destiny was not connected to his own and he accepted this fate, although it did seem unnatural to him. Ana María, on the other hand, did try to change her daughter's mind, only once, when Venezuela wanted to cut her hair, as if to shed an old skin, just as Leona Coralina had done long ago when she left Colombia.

"*Mi amor*," she told her daughter, "you are already getting rid of a city, your parents, and your books. At least keep your hair."

The day before her departure, at the time when the orioles were still sleeping, Venezuela was finishing packing her suitcase while Ana María was reading a newspaper, when they saw a woman come down from the mango tree in the garden with the languor of a sloth. It was the ghost of an Indian woman, covered in dust and dirt, with scraped knees and leaves stuck to her hands, who jumped down from the lowest branches and crossed the garden, leaving behind a smell of old bark. Venezuela followed her with her eyes without a word, her mouth agape, but it was Ana María who recognized her first:

"That's Mute Teresa," she said. "She has come down from her tree at last."

The Indian woman made a timid gesture with her head, as if to say hello, but continued on her way without appearing to know who they were. She went through the living room, the two corridors, opened the front door, and stepped out without having said a single word. Venezuela, still transfixed in surprise, turned to Ana María, who commented serenely under her breath, still concentrating on her newspaper, "It seems everyone wants to leave this house."

The next day, at the Grano de Oro Airport, Venezuela did not shed a tear as she said goodbye to her mother and father, promising to return with her heart full of new languages and ancient cultures. She was going to Caracas, seeking adventure, convinced that she would be able to get a scholarship and maybe one day reach Paris. Ana María knew that she would never come back, that her destiny would be played out elsewhere, she knew better than anyone that travel is like an irresistible magnet, that it draws into itself the hungriest souls, those who can measure up to it, but she said nothing. Antonio, despite his severity, wept in silence, for he could not help imagining all the dangers that might lie in wait for her innocence, and felt as if he was surrendering his daughter to the minotaurs.

She boarded the plane with mixed feelings of excitement and bitterness. Displaying courage as exemplary as her father's when he had left Santa Rita for the Majestic, tenacity as blind as her mother's when she had set out for the university, and madness as intense as her brother's when he had responded to the inner call of black magic,

Venezuela flew up into the sky as her eyes followed the contours of the hills, the departing canoes heading down south, loaded with luggage and birdcages, with suitcases and sacks of corn flour, and contemplated Maracaibo one last time with its twinkling lights still glinting through the caravans of clouds.

Antonio was more saddened by Venezuela's departure from the house on Avenida 3H than Ana María was, but the events that would really change him had not yet taken place. He never understood precisely how his daughter's departure happened to coincide with an upheaval in his life that was much more significant than the one provoked by the spill from the Barroso well of the Venezuelan Oil Concession fifty years earlier. As he was returning home, after a night on call, he passed in front of the little run-down University of Maracaibo and noticed that it was now in ruins, surrounded by drooping palm trees. At the entrance, against one of the columns of the porch, he saw a donkey attached by a rope grazing on the dry grass, on which someone had hung a sign saying: "Rector of the university."

Maracaibo was living through a period of prosperity so intense that, in the frenzy, no one had thought about education. Nobody suspected that Maracaibo could wind up like Potosí after the plunder by the Spanish, or Cubagua after all the pearl oyster beds were ransacked, or Easter Island after the trees were cut down, even poorer and sadder than it was before. The only triumph of intelligence, that temple intended to build the generations of tomorrow, now resembled a felled oak tree in the middle of a scene of pillage. The destiny of cities is often the fruit of a thousand random occurrences. Such was the situation when the tragedy of the airplane crash inspired Antonio with the desire to reconstruct the university.

One March 16th, around midday, a Viasa airline plane heading for Miami crashed a few minutes after takeoff. In those days, the only airport in Maracaibo was called Grano de Oro and was laid out in all its glory in the middle of the city, surrounded by residential areas on all four sides. The aircraft lost control and fell onto the roofs of La Trinidad, provoking a gigantic explosion that was visible from the other side of town. The tragedy caused eighty-four deaths in the air and seventy-one on the ground. The airport of Grano de Oro was permanently shut down that very day and the vast area of land, with its long straight runways, remained abandoned in the city center like a desert island in the middle of the ocean. Antonio, who was unaware of the destiny that awaited him, was finishing an operation when he heard the news about the tragedy. But it was only when the closing of the airport was announced on all the radio stations that an idea came to him with blinding clarity.

"That is where we need to sow light."

The accident, which shook the whole world, marked a turning point in Antonio's life. He could see the possibility of transforming the Grano de Oro airport, which was ideally located, into a new university. With the same determination that had consumed him when he had decided to go from selling Henri Reille's cigarettes to becoming a porter on the docks, he resolved to change hats and become a rector rather than a doctor.

He was already a man in his sixties, with tired skin on which the difficulties of a long existence had left a few visible marks. He had rigid features, a slightly hunched posture, weaker shoulders than in the past, but had kept the cavernous, authoritarian voice that had made him one of the most respected men in the country. Antonio started thinking about this opportunity while he was still in his position at the hospital, and for the first time in the peaceful course of his years in medicine, he became obsessed with a certainty.

When night fell, he walked over the deserted field of Grano de Oro, saw the powdery, deserted landing strips, examined with almost academic interest the ancient splendor of the ruined airport, the old buildings with broken windows, the control towers like solitary belfries, the rusty fences, and the tufts of weeds covering the cement, all of which seemed razed by the tragedy of the accident. Antonio then imagined a gleaming new campus full of students, with libraries filling the aisles of the old terminal, green lawns covering the parking lots, lecture halls where the air-traffic spaces once were, and this outlandish idea provoked in him such enthusiasm, such internal agitation that he had a premonitory dream that very night.

He spent the night convinced that Maracaibo was about to give birth to its finest child, a city within the city, a metropolis with walls made of books. He dreamed of a field of magnolia trees, covered in a million flowers, one of which was made of stone. He turned toward the sky above that field and saw three gigantic bronze letters bolted to a wall, three letters that had always been there and that had never resonated with such an echo: LUZ. He woke up with petals scattered between his sheets. Those three letters were already an obsession. They meant "light" but were also an anagram of the first three letters of Zulia. The strength of the name confirmed that his decision was irrevocable.

He told his dream to Ana María, who answered that magnolias are symbols of wisdom, and that all wise men know that one should cultivate one's garden. From that day forward, Antonio could find no rest, for the vision of that dream had obliged him to take up a new challenge. The next day, he had a request for expropriation of the Grano de Oro site drawn up and, document in hand, started looking all through the city for the governor so he could sign it, with the same fervor he had shown in watching for Ana María in the high-school corridors. He found the governor one day during a press conference, speaking about the funds being unblocked for the construction of a freeway, surrounded by an audience of financiers and young entrepreneurs. After his speech, as he was about to get up and leave, the gathering heard a voice resound throughout the room.

"*Gobernador*," said Antonio. "What is missing is the university."

All the heads turned toward Antonio, who lost none of his composure and added, "Freeways must lead to learning."

The governor considered the idea to be an interesting one. He had Antonio join him in an elegant official car and sat next to him with a distrustful smile on his face.

"You have exactly five blocks, two intersections, and three stoplights to tell me about this university."

Antonio told him that he first needed to approve the expropriation decree of the Grano de Oro site and publish it in the *Official Gazette*, in which all the administrative documents of the country were circulated. He pulled out the paper, already typed up, ready to be approved and printed, and handed it to the governor, who glanced at it quickly.

"It says here that the expropriation of the land is valid for five hundred years?"

"Yes, *gobernador*," Antonio replied. "I had the humility not to put it down for a millennium."

The governor was seduced. He changed his destination and sped to the governmental palace. He laid down the document on the desk of his legal department and declared, "Make sure this is printed in the *Gazette*, tonight."

Antonio followed the document's movements through each office of the palace, all the way to the national printing press, where he waited until one in the morning for it to be published. When he at last held in his hands the printed *Gazette* with the decree number 343, his fingers stained with the still-wet ink, the indelible proof that the land of Grano de Oro would be put at the service of his dream, when he read the words "the lands of what will be the zone of the University of Maracaibo are declared to be of public interest," he understood that he now needed a good lawyer.

Don Victor Emiro Montero was then a very old man who had not been weakened by the burdens of justice and the responsibility for a large family. Antonio found him in his office in the center of Maracaibo. He was completely bald, looked like a reed pipe, and was always busy pushing up his round wire-rim glasses from the tip of his nose, but the nobility of his figure had not changed since that evening when Antonio had seen him for the first time in his kitchen. His children had grown up, his wife had died, the oil company belonging to Mister Barton had left the country under the pressure of the first nationalizations, his house had been sold after nine births and three funerals, but it seemed that Don Victor Emiro, with that discreet and tranquil attitude that seemed to slow down time, was continuing to vanquish the years without having to make an effort and was surviving everyone else. Antonio had no need to persuade him. In fact he barely had time to set out the difficult conditions of his suicidal project before Don

Victor Emiro interrupted him and took his hand, his eyes full of admiration: "And there was I thinking you would only be a doctor."

And he added these words with the same symbolic weight as those he had uttered in front of Mister Barton, forty-five years earlier: "You will be a rector."

For Antonio the construction of the university was like the birth of a cathedral. From the very first days, he explored the entire zone himself, accompanied by a geologist and a foreman, followed by an army of carpenters and masons who were already building imaginary walls in their minds, and he hired a group of excavators to dig the foundations and the trenches for the buildings to come. The site was so vast that it included not only the runways of the old airport but also a dozen shantytowns where families were still living. While Don Victor Emiro was drawing up the new boundaries, Antonio gathered thirty young men, bought five cans of paint and twenty stakes, then, under the sweltering midday sun, gave instructions for all the houses to be identified by numbering their doors with a paintbrush one after the other. He then took care to speak with each of the inhabitants himself, sitting at their tables, negotiating the amount of compensation, such that after two weeks, he had managed to convince the very last of them.

But the next day, new shantytowns appeared, built during the night, set up by profiteers who also wanted to obtain compensation. The site managers brought in tractors to destroy these new buildings. Diggers and heavy military trucks came in and turned over the ground, demolished the cardboard walls, broke the fences, towed away the caravans, and this terrible scene, which left an indelible imprint in Antonio's heart, would be reproduced much later, during the revolution, as if in a time loop.

At the end of the month, the site was emptied. Every morning, Antonio would walk over each inch with the care of a jeweler, calculating, checking, inspecting. The first excavations of the soil opened up snake nests scattered all over the two thousand acres like a second city hidden underneath the muddy ground, and the reptiles put up fierce resistance to the tractors and snake charmers who had come with their clarinets and pierced gourds. Antonio, who was not prepared to back down before any adversity, then repeated the words that Simón Bolívar had spoken the day after the declaration of independence, when a tragic earthquake had shaken the new republic, and exclaimed to everyone present: "If nature herself opposes us, we will fight against her and compel her to obey."

Two hundred liters of insecticide were poured onto the ground. Garlic cloves were vaporized, stinking hellebores were planted because their toxicity was said to keep reptiles away, but the only thing that provided real results was an ultrasonic machine brought in from Caracas that made all the snakes as well as the insects within a mile flee. That was not the only surprise. When the snakes decamped, under the thick crust of the Grano de Oro, stones were exhumed with inscriptions in the

Wayuu alphabet, along with coins from the period of Ursúa, a Gypsy grave that contained the bones of thirteen pangolins attached by a rope, and to everyone's surprise, on a hill above a dip in the ground farther to the east, a spring of pure water that the founders of Maracaibo had already mentioned in some Latin texts, the existence of which would later be confirmed when a pre-Columbian codex preserved in Madrid was deciphered.

Antonio bought up the rails abandoned during the Táchira machinists' project to create the checkerboard of the foundations. He ordered two hundred pines to be felled for the doors to his classrooms and had stones brought from Mérida for the arcades of his frontispiece. He mobilized five hundred workmen, thirty-two carpenters, twenty engineers, fifteen architects. It was a project almost comparable to that of Ambrosius Ehinger when he built Maracaibo.

Antonio went home only to sleep for a few hours every night. Rendered mute by overwork, he barely shared the folly of his project with his wife. Ana María, seeing him like this, so absorbed in his task, took his silence for exhaustion and his absence for obstinacy, her heart darkening as she noticed the speed with which her house was growing emptier, month by month, since Venezuela's departure. She told Antonio about this, during a night of insomnia, but he still pursued his dream, deaf to these protests. She resigned herself to observing powerlessly the consequences of this construction project and kept a dignified calm in the face of the metamorphosis of this man who had once, with the same obstinacy, given her a thousand love stories.

Six months had gone by since Venezuela's departure. There was no news of her. Her silence had gone on long enough to start to worry her mother, but Ana María reassured everyone: "When you're nineteen, you don't think about your parents. She'll write soon."

But this serenity was deceptive. Ana María's heart seethed with secret troubles. In the course of the previous weeks, she had secretly sent fifty letters to various family members in Caracas to ask for news. No one knew anything. From that point on, with all the discretion of maternal love, she had drawn on unsuspected reserves of strength in order not to founder into panic, saving what little patience she had left to not jump on a plane and go save her daughter, and this left her with an icy anxiety that later caused her to be bedridden for fifteen years. She took up her habit of talking to spirits again, with the same zeal as when Chinco had succumbed to tetanus, and invited Babel Bracamonte back into her house. He arrived wreathed in black tobacco smoke and pearl necklaces, lit candles that she set to float in glasses of oil to conjure Venezuela's return, and Ana María plunged into such a mystical universe that when a letter from her daughter arrived at the house a year and a half after her departure, she thought that it was a mirage.

Her daughter's letter was in fact the first of a series of forty missives of six pages each, which when set end to end composed a long epistle of a hundred and twenty pages. They must have been lost in the unfathomable labyrinths of the Venezuelan postal services and been accumulating in a pigeonhole on the other side of the country, until they fell into the hands of an astute employee who had forwarded them to the right address.

One fine April day, very early in the morning, a postman had brought a letter from Venezuela to Ana María that had turned the household upside down, not so much because it had been awaited for so long but mostly because it was dated eighteen months previously. The postman returned the next day, and in a short span of time, a great number of letters flowed in from Caracas, arriving all at once at the house on Avenida 3H, while Ana María had been despairing in silence. The following days, new letters arrived in a continuous flood that never slackened, and they soon piled up on the dining-room table without anyone daring to open them. They were all written on the same scented paper, off-white and with a fibrous grain, the fragrance having been miraculously preserved during the long months of waiting in the cold warehouses and post office sorting rooms. They bore the same handwriting, the same hasty gestures, the same melody of nostalgia and promises, such that their only differentiating feature was the date on the top right corner of the envelopes.

Ana María was unaware at the time that Venezuela had been fulfilling her epistolary duty every two weeks, according to an immutable ritual, by the light of a poor candle, with a languishing style that made her wander among her memories of her childhood in Maracaibo, apparently in the conviction that she could bring them back to life with the sole power of her pen.

Ana María thus learned with a year and a half delay about the fascination her daughter felt for the capital. The streets resounded with the echoes of a hundred languages, the stores sold items from all over the world, the squares were flanked by museums, the concert halls received the greatest performers. Each door was a portal to the impossible. Each encounter was an invitation into the unknown. Two weeks of reading were equivalent to two months of life. In November, Ana María would be reading about a love story that took place in March. Venezuela talked about meeting a giant, a man called Octavio, one day in a pharmacy. She had seen him come in, carrying an old wooden table on which his prescription was written, wearing a jacket soiled by coal. His tall stature and wide body had produced in her that yearning created by the sight of men that nothing can subdue.

By the thirtieth letter, they broke open a bottle of champagne when they learned that Venezuela was leaving for Paris. She had obtained a scholarship to go to France. Her dream had become a reality. The family only had to open the envelopes one by one to see her wandering down Saint-Germain-des-Prés, lighthearted and happy, learning French. Her penmanship had become erudite, refined, exquisite. She moved in student circles, could talk about geopolitics and art history, led a life completely opposite to that which had been predestined for her, and always proud of her origins, she talked about her family's stormy past with distinction, as if she were recalling ancient debts.

Then, by the thirty-eighth letter, Venezuela talked about finding love, in a tortured Chilean, a man who had fled Pinochet's dictatorship and had known Pedro Clavel in Santiago. Each of them had left their country to go to another one, to build a kingdom on the other side of the ocean. And there was more than love between them; there was also admiration. Or perhaps also that strange feeling shared by exiles so far from their own lands. Swept up in emotion, she said that when she held him in her arms, she felt powerful, capable of anything, as if she could solve all the problems of the world, because marrying a torture victim from Latin America was already a start in changing it.

While Venezuela was living her Parisian dreams, Antonio was taking the lead of a squadron of builders. During the five years of construction, he hardly slept. He could be seen walking over the entire site, carrying his leather briefcase packed with plans, accompanied by Don Victor Emiro who followed him everywhere, and no one could have said whether it was because of these constant excursions, or the worry caused by the construction, or the lack of sleep, but he started visibly aging, as if this excess of life had accelerated his journey toward death.

Little by little, the buildings started to rise. From that field of ruins harder than limestone, all cracked and abandoned, emerged an academic palace destined to receive the administration of the rectorship, the treasury, and the secretariat. To the north was a group of towering buildings, encircling the sports fields, for the laboratories and research centers. To the south were the arts, humanities, and agronomy faculties and a school specializing in petroleum chemistry. When a group of students, exalted by these rapid developments, crossed the building site and asked when the opening of the university would be announced, Antonio looked up for a while at the erected walls of the new classrooms, their paint still wet, and exclaimed, "The university will be opened when we have written the word 'light' at the entrance."

Three letters in cast copper were brought from Italy: LUZ. They were installed one Tuesday in April, during a commemorative day, in front of an audience of guests, and when Antonio saw those three letters, that name finally inscribed on the frontispiece at the entrance, in huge metallic bars, he felt as if he were living this scene for a second time, for the sparkling memory of the dream he'd had five years earlier came back to him like a gust of wind. Everyone was overawed. The governor himself unfurled garlands of praise for the twenty-two faculties all painted white, the gardens planted with palm trees and ferns, the buildings decorated with bunting. He asked Antonio what mysterious source he had drunk at, what prodigious fire had fed him, in order to imagine such a monument. Antonio replied, with all the simplicity in the world, "It came to me in a dream, *gobernador*."

The doors of the University of Maracaibo were opened for the first time one Monday in May. The emotion with which Antonio spoke to baptize that day, during the inauguration prepared to consecrate its creation and that at the same time marked the end of a titanic building program, proved to everyone that he was the only man in the city capable of bearing the title of rector.

From then onward, he had not a moment's peace for ten years. In the effervescence of this novelty, he concentrated all his energy on the leadership of the faculties, surrounded himself with the finest pedagogical minds in the region, waged a battle to furnish the classrooms with the best equipment, and even had the time to repatriate the remains of the union leader Valmore Rodríguez from Chile to Maracaibo, not so they could be studied in the necrology classes but because he was of the unshakable view that the bones of such a great intellectual could not be left to rest at the other end of the continent.

It was a decade of joys and battles. As well as the faculties, he created twenty-two schools, multiplied the number of pupils by ten, and hired eight hundred teachers. He opened seven research institutes, thirteen educational centers all over Zulia, and to crown this phenomenal success, following the precepts that his master Lossada had long ago passed down to him, he had the words *post nubila phoebus* engraved on the university crest, just as they had once been tattooed in his memory when he was still a schoolboy.

During that same period, Ana María, alarmed by the worrying increase of teenage pregnancies that she could see at the maternity clinic, threw herself into the fight for abortion rights. She was then the head of the well-being services for women at the hospital, influential and respected. She set up a pilot project to carry out surgical abortions on the first floor. Soon the rumor spread. Young women arrived, and it was not long before she discovered that there was a waiting line, starting at five in the morning every day, going all the way around the block. To the head of the hospital who asked for an explanation, Ana María replied, "Women have always had abortions, señor. With or without the law. And they will continue to do so."

But the Ministry of Health learned of the existence of these plans. The first floor was closed down. Ana María, not ready to give up and risking arrest, reopened the service in her own home. Her bedroom with mirrors, built in the couple's great moments of glory, where she and Antonio had once made love like two jaguars, was transformed into a clandestine operating theater filled with metallic instruments, sterilized tweezers and speculums, scissors and cervix brushes, where two midwives were kept busy, paid under the table, coming and going with basins of boiling water. The garden of monsteras, which had been abandoned since Venezuela's departure and the construction of the university, was now filled with young women waiting patiently in silence, holding their bellies in both hands, their eyes lost in the void, clutching a few banknotes in their fists, shaking with fear and shame, their hearts eaten up with remorse.

In the middle of this commotion, Ana María was in a state of constant agitation. She attended each examination, conducted each intervention, but she was so absorbed by her task that she did not see her own mother's death coming.

Eva Rosa slipped away one morning, while the orioles were singing in the mango tree in the garden, on October 8th, her birthday, thus confirming the lore that only pure beings die on the same day as their birth. Her body was so tiny, so light, that it was hard to believe she had actually existed. Her death was one of elegant discretion, just as her life had been. Before she left the world, she had the courtesy of taking care of all the bureaucracy of her own death. A few hours after her passing, a funeral services car parked in silence in front of the house on Avenida 3H to take away the body in a coffin with no handles, and nothing more was seen of her until the day when Ana María, who was wandering by chance in El Cuadrado cemetery, came across her name engraved on a flat stone.

It was at around this time that Antonio left his position as rector. He refused the chair that was offered him, renounced all the directorships, abandoned his title of president of the College of Medicine, and took off both his academic gown and white coat for good. He gave up all his official activities and started roaming around his home like a lone wolf. He didn't leave the house on Avenida 3H. Taking up his place in his former life, Antonio did not notice that he had grown old until the morning when, as he slid into his bathrobe that had been hanging on a hook for more than fifteen years, he realized that it was much too big for him. He had the sudden feeling of having been chased out of his own youth.

After one hundred days of cloistering himself in his mirrored bedroom, his hands shriveled up and his back became stooped. Ana María explained this as the result of a life of duties and obligations, of the imperatives that had shattered his strength, and of the troubling encounter between a man and a country. When she came home, she would find him sitting in his hammock in the back courtyard, staring at the door wreathed with carnations through which the child Pedro Clavel had once entered, holding a cup of coffee in one hand, resting in the middle of the monstera leaves and the bougainvillea vines as if he had been born of this garden, of this silence, of this serenity, so old that no one could ever have imagined that this man had done anything else in his life besides contemplating the void while drinking coffee.

She decided he needed a change of scene. She decreed that instead of staying in Maracaibo, in their house on Avenida 3H, and looking after the flowers, they would go to their other house, Alegría, the one in La Rosita, where Antonio had once found the strength to build a hospital on an island. But when she arrived, she was forced to hang on to the fence to not collapse. That old house, which she had transformed into a serene and blooming paradise, had been worn away by neglect from the inside like a rotten apple and was now no more than a refuge for insects and raccoons, with broken windows and cracked tiles. The impossible blue from the Ishtar Gate was now an abominable washed-out green, the golden spiders had taken possession of every hole in the walls, the geckos had formed a tyrannical colony, and in the bathroom she discovered a crocodile sleeping in the bottom of the tub, its jaws open, with a plover cleaning its teeth and pecking at its gums.

Seized all of a sudden by a new surge of vitality, she decided to give this house the same rebirth she wished for Antonio. She had the plaster on the walls replaced, unhooked the drapes and the net curtains in order to get rid of the dust and parasites, had the floors recovered with large checkerboard pavers, and replaced the sideboard by hanging shelves on which she set out indoor plants and crockery.

One day, Ana María arrived at the door with a team of carpenters and masons who restored the roof, changed the doors, repaired the lights that the storms had smashed, and whitewashed the walls with sodium crystals, so that three weeks after their return, the house Alegría seemed to have been built that very day. The living room was filled with tropical plants and the bedrooms were entirely repainted in yellow to attract the light. She had two fishermen come to dislodge the crocodile from the bathtub, and once it was empty, she decided not to use it to bathe in but to store all the bottles of champagne that she had been given after fifty years of celebrity and not had time to drink.

When she was finished with the house, she took care of her husband. She prepared generous meals for him, concoctions of pomegranate juice for his fragile bladder, shark-liver oil for sleep, but it became clear that despite all her goodwill, the weight of the years had fallen upon him. Antonio would only eat yogurt, plantains with cheese, and a little cereal in a bowl of milk, which made him lose so much weight that he started believing that his old jackets, pants, and shoes, his suspenders, and his underpants all belonged to another man, one much taller and fatter, who had lived in the same house before him. Since he could not sleep at night, he was always exhausted during the day.

That was why he heaved a sigh of fatigue when, one morning in 1986, he received the announcement that he should attend the inauguration of the plaque on the street that was to bear his name. This news provoked a fit of lumbago that lasted six weeks.

This occurred on Friday, December 22nd. Around midday, all Maracaibo was present when Antonio stepped onto the dais to inaugurate this new plaque. He'd had a haircut, a shave, and wore the same suit he had worn on the day of the investiture of the rectorship, but Antonio, caught in the trap of his own memories, could not rid himself of nostalgia. During the whole morning, in the oven-like heat on the pavement, he was more tormented by the twilight afterglow of his life than by the honors that were being bestowed upon him, for he had reached a threshold of indifference to glory and been liberated at last from the burden of his dreams, and there now remained in the back of his mouth only an insistent taste of ancient ashes. There was a fanfare, popped balloons filled with confetti, ovations and acclamations, and at that highly symbolic moment of his career, he could not help himself from thinking back to his childhood in Pela el Ojo and to the dog that had followed him swimming into the lake, the day he had stolen the boat belonging to Asdrubal Urribarri.

He managed not to fall asleep during the interminable speech by the governor, who drew up a list of his distinctions and diplomas, and recalled his modest origins, but during this time, in silence, Antonio could not shake off the memory of Leona Coralina, who had shaved her head to preserve a semblance of dignity under the red lights of the Majestic. He saw once again the delicate face of Don Victor Emiro Montero in his kitchen as he read the letter from Elías, and he felt nostalgia for that time when it was simpler to be a man.

Applause pulled him out of his reverie and he was brought to a Ford automobile to drive down the new street. As he stepped through the car door, he thought about all those people who had left an enduring footprint in the cement of his youth, and realized how much he had loved his childhood in which violence had been met with courage. The car moved off and a few dogs started running after it. His name rang out several times through the city's loudspeakers, as if this was the procession of a cardinal, but all he heard was the distant laugh of Ana María. In a marvelous vision, he distinguished her pregnant figure in a robe, in the corridors of their house, bearing in her body his only true masterpiece.

At one-thirty a band with copper clarinets and goatskin drums played a *gaita* at an intersection, but he paid no attention to it. Only the brilliant evening of January 23, 1958, was shining inside him, when he arrived late for his only child's birth.

Throughout the duration of the drive, he thought about his daughter, Venezuela, on the other side of the ocean, who was about to have a baby herself, and he wondered whether he was in fact already a grandfather. This evocation led him to think in spite of himself about his own birth, as did all the memories that had endured the squalls of his years. When he passed in front of the church, he had a fond thought for Mute Teresa, for at the moment when the car was going around a corner, he saw the steps on which he had been left on the third day of his life and he understood that, at the very beginning of everything, that woman who was not his mother had saved him from not having a mother at all. The car turned, continuing its journey through the applauding crowds, and the church fell into the background. Before it disappeared forever in the throng of children and dogs, Antonio saw the ghost of his father, Elías Borjas Romero, who died in a gloomy hovel in the company of prostitutes and drunks, that nomadic sailor who, eighty years ago, had abandoned his son on the steps of misery after hiding a cigarette rolling machine in the folds of his blanket, then set off on his ship *El Nautilus*, bathed in tears and singing Cuban boleros as he left the port of Maracaibo.

Antonio was dropped off at a street corner where journalists, dignitaries, politicians, and performers were waiting for him. He was asked to pull on the little curtain to unveil the plaque. Antonio was so old, so exhausted, that he was unable to raise his arm and someone had to do it for him. When the curtain fell, his poor eyesight did not allow him to read what was written on the plaque. But he knew at that instant that what was engraved there, on the stone of the present, was the name of the past.

Cristóbal

Cristóbal was born in Paris on the day when the street bearing the name of Antonio Borjas Romero was inaugurated in Maracaibo. He came into the world during the coldest winter in France, when the wind outside was making bridges crack and stones split, and the air was so icy that it broke the grass in the parks like glass needles. The cry he let out as he came into the world, on one side of the ocean, was similar to the chisel blows being hammered into the marble of the plaque by the artisans on the other side. Those blows put a seal on one existence and opened up another. Eighty years apart, one had already carried the world, while the other knew nothing of its weight, and this cry rising out of generations from the one entering life, which Venezuela was giving through her blood and pain, could be found in the echo of the infant's grandfather who, at the same instant, was entering history.

A few years previously, it was at the gates of Paris, in the Bois de Vincennes, between the red oaks from America and the nut trees from Byzantium, that Venezuela had met the man by whom she would become pregnant. At that time, she had a mix of tropical and European manners, an exoticism in her expressions, a floral accent in whichever language she spoke that set men off onto lustful voyages. She dined with painters and writers, ministers and diplomats, and had developed social graces that endowed her with the reputation of a refined woman. In those elitist circles, where family names and genealogies were everything, the pertinence of her words, her rare taste, and the courage of her choices allowed her origins to be forgiven. Despite the rhythm of her social life, with its charmed evenings and gallant parties, she aspired to the burrows of a serene love.

That was why she never would have imagined that on that particular Sunday, when a friend invited her to watch a soccer game in the Bois de Vincennes, and she was dragging her feet about going there, she would fall in love with the team's captain, an exile from the Chilean dictatorship, a man whose body had been tortured in the most sinister jails of Santiago, who was much younger than she was, and who was at present running after the ball with the eagerness of an excited puppy. Venezuela had barely sat down in the bleachers when she saw him, and it took her only a minute to surrender to the oceanic thunderbolt of love at first sight, knowing at once that she would teach this man to find again all the beauty that the dictatorship had erased inside him.

His name was Ilario Da. After his forced exile from Chile, to protect himself, he had changed his name at the French border to Michel René, and Venezuela started tenderly calling him Michel Da. When she first met him, Ilario Da didn't have a cent to his name nor a diploma in his hands, but his cheerfulness and charm gave him the wealth of character. He was a Mirist, in other words a member of MIR, an extreme left-wing revolutionary movement in Chile, and he pronounced that word with such assuredness that he seemed to be presenting himself as a prophet. His life was the perfect opposite of hers.

He lived in a tiny garret room on the seventh floor, without an elevator, wrote books, was a stage manager at the neighborhood theater, and spent all his evenings at tables in bars planning his clandestine return to Chile, hidden in the hold of a ship, armed to the teeth, to bring down the dictator and take the Moneda de Santiago just as Che had done, ten years earlier in Havana.

However, this fighter's old dream, this illusion of a heroic return to continue the workers' struggle, this mirage remained nothing but a chimera for the rest of his life, for his encounter with Venezuela made him start another revolution, that of having a family. He soon had season tickets to the Paris Opera, got a job in a perfumery in a rich neighborhood, became the owner of a house in the suburbs, and sat at the tables of ambassadors and government emissaries, the very ones he had fought in the past. It was not so much that he turned his back on his cause, and never until the day he died did he lose the clarity of his convictions, but love had won the battle over politics, and he quickly resigned himself to the fact that his return to his native land was no more than an illusion. He accepted living in comfort, admitted the advantages that his relationship offered him, and allowed himself the frivolous pleasures of the bourgeoisie, while all the time repeating that he would never be right-wing. The day he married Venezuela, at the *mairie* of the eleventh arrondissement one August morning, he insisted that "The Internationale" be sung under the dome.

Cristóbal was born in the cold of December from those two migrants. Ilario Da was an atheist, faithful to the old anarchist idea that there should be neither God nor masters. But Venezuela insisted she was Catholic and intended to have the child baptized according to the rituals of her faith.

"For even if there is no God, there will always be a master somewhere," she said with composure.

She had nothing against Allende or class warfare, but she refused to have her child named Salvador or Karl and was even more adamant that he should not be given a Russian name. Ilario Da, who quickly understood that one of the secrets of a happy couple is to choose one's battles, capitulated in the face of her intransigence, for he had guessed that it was pointless to stand up to this tenacious and bewitching young woman with black eyes who smelled of orchids, with whom he now shared his life.

This is how the child came to be named Cristóbal, in honor of the man who carried Christ and the one who brought the church to America. However, Ilario Da insisted he be educated in secular French schools, categorically forbade any church attendance on Sundays, and demanded that they speak Spanish at home and that they should wait for him to turn sixteen before telling him about the horrors of dictatorship. Venezuela accepted, for this man whose body was as long and slim as a panther's, with rough hands and white chest hair, had already renounced a Latin American revolution for her, and in marriage as in life, everything is a matter of compromise.

Cristóbal was not yet five when he learned to read. This discovery channeled his energy. At ten, no matter what time Venezuela saw him in the house, he was always buried to his shoulders in a book, looking down, his chin to his chest, absorbed in his reading. Because he was both Latin American and European, he was bathed in a mythology located on the border between two continents, two cultures, two languages, of which he was the result. He was fascinated by the stories of the adventurers who had long ago disembarked in America. He memorized the beliefs about the discovery of the New World, the treasures of Montezuma, the seven cities of Cíbola, and King Solomon's mines, the unclean people of Gog and Magog, the palace with gold tiles in Cipangu and the cities of silver of Paititi, such that he reached the age of twelve unaware of anything to do with dictatorships or migrations, revolts or pogroms, but with his imagination bursting with Cyclopes and saints, similar to that of a colonist in New Amsterdam.

All of these stories were so wild and fantastical that they held him with the same magnetic power that had once attracted the conquistadors. And so new maps were drawn in his mind that would later impel him to cross the ocean to rejoin his parents' past. Portolanos were drafted in his memory, floating on figures of sea snakes, on which Maracaibo was a lake of petroleum where mixed-race sirens lived, where the fountain of youth hid the tomb of the apostle Thomas, and where a handful of men who knew nothing of the language of pumas or of clay, five centuries previously, had managed to vanquish the kings of Indigenous empires.

Cristóbal's voracity encouraged him to learn more about a world he believed to be his, the world of his ancestors, the world of his blood. His reading drove him to plains of dolphin women and rivers shaped like salamanders, to swamps where the fish were said to have gold scales and where the trees grew upside down.

But when he looked up from the page, all Cristóbal could see was a suburban house and a backyard of gravel and garage doors. His books smelled of mangoes and bougainvillea; his life smelled of the plane tree in the street. He searched the neighbor's balcony for Pizarro's land of cinnamon and the accounts of Magellan's impossible expeditions. Alone, drunk with the splendors of the past, he would imagine the virulent power with which the domes of Madrid had resonated with the rumor of cardinals asking, in a language eroded by Latin and octosyllables, whether the conquistadors of Patagonia had really seen the nation of giants.

While Cristóbal was growing up in a universe of cosmogonies, Venezuela was appointed the cultural counselor of the embassy of her country. Now a diplomat, she started traveling from capital to capital, from country to country, representing her homeland abroad, thus accomplishing the same task as the chroniclers of the Western Indies had on their return from America. From then on, Cristóbal's childhood was only a series of moves and journeys, displacement and uprooting. His perpetual travels were at first a constant wrench, a disorder in his heart, but they also allowed him to have his first encounter with immobility.

It was a novel. He started it during one of his many journeys with his parents, and very quickly, submerged in his reading, without raising his eyes, he forgot all about the airports and the railway stations, the trains and the suitcases, for he had read the book all the way to the end without realizing it, without paying any attention to the people around him, without noticing his exhaustion. When the plane landed, as he turned the last page, Cristóbal's throat was tight, his eyes wet, and his soul was cleft in two between envy and wonder. Seeing her son's emotion, Venezuela had said, "To read is to travel."

But for Cristóbal, whose childhood was nothing but movement, to read was to stay still. The cities changed, the languages multiplied, the cultures flew past his eyes one after the other, but the books were the same. Whether they went to Lisbon, Rome, Caracas, or Buenos Aires, the novels of his youth did not change. He remained close to his books as one might remain close to animals and stroke their heavy manes. Their boards with covers as silky as fur and the familiar fonts of their titles brought him more reassuring appeasement than did the names of countries. To read is not to travel. Pages have the immobility of metal or agate. Cristóbal would set out for these petrified realms, plunge into their geometries of ink and grain, lose himself in their labyrinths only to find himself once more, crashing each time against the same masts of their beauty. That was where the invariable foundations of men lay, the place of refuge where they could rest from chaos, a safe haven with no departures or exile. Novels are an island surrounded with land.

This was the situation when the coup d'état that would change the history of Venezuela occurred. His father, Ilario Da, was the first to hear about it. He rushed into their Parisian home one evening at dinnertime when Cristóbal and Venezuela were in the kitchen and started shouting with the same crazed voice as the workers of the Venezuelan Oil Concession had before the gusher of oil.

"Revolution! Revolution!"

They turned on the television. In Caracas, military revolutionaries had decided to seize power and were fighting a relentless battle in the streets of the capital. This earthquake lasted twenty-four hours, unleashing a furious crowd scene and Dantesque disorder. But although that day was like a cataclysm, it was not the first time that such events had shaken the country. There had already been as many revolutions as wars in Venezuela.

In two centuries, it had known some hundred slave insurrections and popular revolts, from José Leonardo Chirino to the Caracazo, some fifty uprisings for independence before Bolívar, including those of Manuel Gual and José María España. The Blue Revolution was followed by the April Revolution, which was itself supplanted by the Coro Revolution. In two centuries, there had already been thousands of armed peasant groups under Ezequiel Zamora, of infantries emerging out of farms, of agrarian reforms and battles against the latifundista. In two centuries, between decrees and their implementation, there had been almost thirty constitutions written, armies of guerrilleros under the banner of Fabricio Ojeda, hundreds of union movements leading to national strikes, a dozen coups d'état, both civil and military. In two centuries, the Venezuelan people had so loved liberty that they had become its slave.

That was why, on February 4, 1992, when a few young soldiers, inspired by collective memory, attempted a revolution in the middle of the night, it came as a surprise to nobody. It was the fruit of a long battle against servitude that had been biding its time and had come from much further back, as if exhumed from oblivion by ancient forces, one that had been on the march ever since the day when Samuel Smith had not been able to contain the gusher from the Barroso well, since the day when the first foreign companies swallowed all the wealth into themselves, since the day when Chinco fought against the Gómez regime, since the day when Ana María committed herself to fighting the dictatorship of Pérez Jiménez, since the day when Antonio was tortured in the jails of the Cuartel Libertador. And yet this revolution, shaped from the clay of a series of frustrations and abuses, would end up, like the others before it, unwittingly reproducing precisely what it had set out to fight.

In the house on Avenida 3H, that February 4th, in Maracaibo, four hundred miles from the capital, the first signs of the uprising could be felt with distant virulence. Ana María noticed it in the cleaning ladies' nervousness and the tumult in the air that suddenly became agitated. She heard the clicking of weapons in each crinkle of the curtains, the murmur on the streets in each rustle of the sheets, the anguish of the teeming city in each pillow feather, and she had the sense that she was reliving that magnificent and terrifying afternoon when she had given birth to her daughter in the middle of a coup d'état. She turned on the television and had to put her head down so as not to faint when she saw the images of a tank, in Caracas in the middle of the day, climbing up the steps of the presidential palace to break down the main doors.

War broke out between the revolutionaries and the governmental army. The country ground to a halt, stupefied, observing this rift tearing open the fabric of its history. Ana María, her mouth agape in front of her television, then remembered the prophetic words of her father, Chinco Rodríguez, who, on the morning when the police had come to take him away after a denunciation, had left this little note on his nightstand: "The day of the revolution will come."

But the revolution did not come. The coup of February 4th failed. The army quashed this formidable mutiny and arrested those who had fomented it. Therefore no one could precisely remember the events of that day, nor the number of dead, nor the fear freighted in each bullet that was shot, but the country would long remember the face of a thirty-eight-year-old man, wearing a red beret and a country suit, his hands handcuffed behind his back, and whose skin color had something of the mixed-race people of Llanos, who was exhibited in front of all the world's televisions as the principal architect of the rebellion.

"For now," he said, "we have not succeeded. For now."

He was dragged through the city to be escorted to Yare Prison, where he would be locked up for two years. The military police would later say that, during the trip, a shower of applause had accompanied the rebel as he passed by. Ana María followed this scene from miles away, from her mirrored bedroom in Maracaibo, and she then felt that something alarming had just been born. Yesterday, that boy was nobody. Today, he was everybody.

And the country was unaware that this man who would found a party and become president of the republic six years later would also be the one to set off one of the most violent crises that would lead to the exile of millions of its citizens.

Antonio was one of the few people who did not allow themselves to be too distressed by this affair. At that time, he rose before dawn despite himself and sat on his bed for an hour, in silence, checking through the interminable list of the pains assailing his body. He would go into his kitchen to drink a cup of coffee, which was the only one of all the guilty pleasures remaining in his life that his doctor still allowed him. He would then settle into his hammock, wearing shorts and a T-shirt, on his patio filled with flower pots, and sink into a half sleep that exhausted him even more, then go back into his bedroom when the heat of midday chased him away and the cramps in his stomach became unbearable, to lie on his bed, worn out from the day, as speechless as Mute Teresa. Deaf to the rumor of the coup d'état and political upheavals, all Antonio could understand was that the secret of a happy death was first to have decided on it.

This decision was like a decree. He had arrived at the conclusion that the most precious gift of existence was the possibility of stopping it as one pleased. The certainty of his death came to him all of a sudden. He was not surprised by it, for he had lived long enough to know his body's limits, but he realized that his desire to be over and done with it had come earlier than he had imagined. One Wednesday, when he had locked himself in the bathroom for an hour, looking dispassionately at the walls filled with dusty old diplomas and honorific distinctions, with their initial letters blooming with arabesques, on which the ashen cherubs were the only remains of his past, he saw his face in the reflection on the glass of one of the frames and had trouble recognizing the expression in his own eyes. He saw his forehead, as wrinkled as a mountain of melted cheese, and his nose, as withered as a faded flower, and he understood that he was ready not to see himself anymore, because he had arrived at an age when one no longer misses oneself.

And so he left the bathroom, crossed the house dragging his feet, and went out into the garden and told Ana María, who was sitting in the shade, that he had resolved to die and that this was the last decision of his life, for he would take no other beyond that.

"I can't even remember how to piss."

Ana María, who had never lost her nerve in the most difficult situations, turned toward her husband, unmoved. She fondly observed how the rains of life had eroded the skin of this man, who had been considered in his youth as one of the most attractive of his generation, and of which now remained only a tired old wolf. But she found him handsome in his exhaustion, noble in his simplicity, and it was all she could do to answer, "Don't worry, it'll come back to you."

No one paid any attention to Antonio's resolution to leave the world according to his own will. By chance, only one journalist in Maracaibo, Alfredo Mercurio Bustamante, learned the news as he was drinking a glass of coffee in the café on the square. Surprised by this announcement, he forwarded it to his newspaper and titled his article: "The Immortal Who Decided to Die."

The rumor spread throughout the whole region, from the roads snaking up the hillsides to the depths of the territory of Zulia, and relegated all breaking news to the background. The tank on the steps of the presidential palace, the collapse of a radio tower, the trials in progress, none of that was news in that part of the world and dozens of people started gathering in front of the house on Avenida 3H to catch a glimpse of the most famous doctor of Maracaibo who had decided, while he still had all his wits, to die in peace.

Some of them came to see him to try to persuade him to renounce his intention, others brought him notes folded into four for him to give to their deceased loved ones. There were so many visitors who joined that line of strangers that the doors and windows of the house had to be shut to avoid any incidents, but Antonio opened them again with authority and declared that only animals wished to die alone. Toward midday, the house was so packed, there was so little space left in the living room, that a child accidentally knocked over an Oriental amphora with his elbow, one that Ana María had ordered from Yemen. His mother was reprimanding him with violence, when Antonio appeared in the living room, and with a calm and assured gesture, seized a second amphora and smashed it to smithereens on the floor.

"Madam," he declared, "in this house children are more important than objects."

At that moment, the neighbor Zina, leaving her chair on the porch where she had been waiting for her French producer for a hundred years, came into the living room and, of all the people present, was perhaps the only one to attempt to dissuade him.

"It's a crime to commit suicide, Antonio."

To which Antonio replied, "My only crime is to have stayed alive for so long. I think I've done my time."

In the beginning of the afternoon, he had his hairdresser come into his bedroom to spend two hours grooming him for his encounter with God, as well as his barber, who gave him a close shave, in case the journey was longer than expected. He ordered for all his personal effects to be delivered to the hospital where he had spent almost thirty years of his life, washed the walls, and called his tailor to come make him a custom-made suit. When he went out of the house a few hours later, combed like a prince and wearing a magnificent linen suit, several people remarked that he had never been seen looking so splendid since the day that his street was inaugurated. In the certainty of his will, he asked to be driven to the cemetery in his own car, and with the precise and authoritative gestures that had made him famous during the founding of the university, he chose the location of his grave himself. When he got home, he set the time of his death for that evening, but only after dinner, for he considered, like Mama Concha many years beforehand, that it was a bad omen to die on an empty stomach. He ate some *pabellón criollo*, pulled beef with rice and black beans, for the last time in his life and had the impression that the meat tasted like the reeds of Santa Rita.

While Ana María was smoking her pipe outside, Antonio changed into his robe and walked around his garden to fill the water tubs for the monsteras. He noticed the rolled-up leaves that would be born in a few days and regretted not being able to see them. Then after clearing the table himself and brushing his teeth, he lay down on his bed, still surrounded by the mirrors that had stayed there since they had moved in, and closed his eyes. In the middle of this annunciatory darkness, he felt himself gently slip to the depths of the lake, in an underwater corridor that had been decorated with medals, as if he were diving into the belly of Maracaibo, without knowing that there, at the bottom, death was waiting for him. Antonio died alone, but Ana María knew it immediately, for at that instant, on the other side of the house, as she was serving herself a glass of tamarind juice, she found a trace of bitter ash at the bottom of the jug.

"Antonio is gone," she said aloud.

Without getting up, she measured the magnitude of her loneliness for the first time and wondered whether this new feeling foretold her own death. She still had the will to live, but her heart sank further in the knowledge that she was now deprived of the serenity of love. She thought back to that period of rest, under the pergola of the house on Avenida 3H, when they had made love so feverishly, and to that bus trip home when the soldiers had ordered them out, and to January 23, 1958, when he was given his freedom at the same moment as she went into labor, and all those memories plunged her into a profound melancholy.

Venezuela learned the news a few hours later, five thousand miles away, on the other side of the Atlantic, in her house in Malakoff on the outskirts of Paris.

The telephone had rung. She was told everything. The funeral would be held in three days. Cristóbal was deep in a book, concentrating on the stories of man-eaters and the city of the Caesars, when his mother, Venezuela, hung up the phone, and without saying a word, wept softly in front of a mirror. Her eyes swollen with tears, she took him into her arms.

"I'm leaving tomorrow for Maracaibo. You're coming with me."

It never occurred to him that this trip to Latin America, this flight toward his origins, would also be his first journey into himself. When Cristóbal packed his suitcase, under the pressure of his mother's haste, he put in the books about the chronicles of the Indies and the navigations of Pigafetta, and he crossed the ocean on the plane of a French airline on which chardonnay was served to accompany Lyon quenelles.

He landed in a world of banana groves and unfinished freeways, in unbearable heat, and the first thing that surprised him was the strong stench of fuel that hung in the air of Maracaibo. From the car that took them to the house on Avenida 3H, he could see the white facades of the buildings blackened by the smoke of memories and the dust of the past, the dogs drinking from the gutters, the women sitting in the shade, protecting themselves from the heat thanks to a thousand tricks passed down from generation to generation, the Dominican friars on the squares who still wrote love letters for ten cents, the American sedans driving alongside the carts drawn by blue donkeys, and he wondered if these were the same donkeys that had once transported the eleven thousand pounds of gold for the ransom of Atahuallpa.

These contrasting sights, which had nothing to do with what he had imagined, and which both disappointed and attracted him at the same time, crossed his mind as if they were a new novel to discover. Everything became material. He did not yet know that writing would become a biological necessity for him. That day, in the back of that car, he could not grasp the scope of what surrounded him, even when he passed the old port where long ago, almost a century previously, the soiled statue of Simón Bolívar had been set down, around which Antonio Borjas Romero's dreams were formed.

At midday, Cristóbal was let into the house through the garden door entirely covered with brambles and roses, where Pedro Clavel had once been crowned with a shower of carnations. He understood that he was in his mother's childhood home, for the postcards of Paris were still hanging on the walls and, in the confusion of dozens of people coming and going for the funerary vigil, he thought he recognized familiar faces she had shown him in an old album she had taken out of a trunk one distant French Sunday.

While Venezuela was talking to strangers in the corridor, Cristóbal had to wait in the white hammock in the garden, where Antonio had sat during his last years, contemplating the monsteras all around him with their now open leaves and the tubs of bougainvillea vines that Eva Rosa had watered every morning, cooling herself with a fan to fend off the mosquitoes made feverish by the heat. He examined the branches of the mango tree, under which Mute Teresa had been buried with seeds in her mouth, and was wondering about the mysteries that this house held within itself, when his mother came to take him by the hand and pulled him into a room that for fifty years had been his grandparents'.

Two nuns were praying in the middle of the room, sitting on a wooden bench. They did not get up when Cristóbal entered. In the silvering of the mirrors into which nobody had looked since Antonio's death and in the old curtains worn by neglect, a silence had settled that was so palpable, so thick, that Cristóbal could have squeezed it between his two hands. This master bedroom, which was once the most sparkling and ornate in the whole city, now had the haunting odor of old bric-a-brac. Venezuela held his arm until they reached the back wall where Antonio's body lay. As she drew near, she could not stifle a voiceless sob.

"Here is your grandfather," she said. "The eternal rector."

Cristóbal, who knew nothing about this man, cast a slanting glance at his little old body as if he were a wax statue, and scanned his pallid skin and emaciated cheekbones, but nothing could lead him to imagine that this inanimate, numb face could once have lived a life of such brilliance. This figure reminded him of the descriptions of Patagonians he had read in the Dutch accounts of Sebald de Weert, who told of bodies so large that their fists could hold a bull. Cristóbal felt something akin to what the adventurers had felt when they discovered the relics of an imaginary past, but he was not able to put words to that feeling until later, until the day that he would decide to write this story.

The funeral was set for the first Saturday of July. Maracaibo then experienced one of the most anticipated ceremonies of all time. From the upper-class neighborhoods to the poorest suburbs, from the heights of the sierra to the docks of the old port, a long procession of strangers, of ordinary people, their heads bowed in grief, with horses with black ribbons braided into their tails, filed in front of the coffin to the sound of a slow funeral march, while Venezuela lit candles in the shape of doves. Antonio was buried with all his medals and diplomas, and his coffin was filled with so many mementos, his pockets with so many amulets and talismans, that it took eight pallbearers to carry it. The statues of San Benito and Saint Luke were also brought out and carried in a heavy parade around the square, and musicians played ballads about a sailor marrying the sea.

The bells of the cathedral rang all the changes, and the ceremony lasted four hours without a break. No one had ever had such a funeral in Maracaibo. The sky was filled with immense sadness. The body was let down into the grave and covered in flowers, and Antonio remained enclosed in the earth forever more, like those Greek statues that fall during battles, leaving behind a memory of greatness and cracked marble.

The death of Antonio foretold Ana María's. Just as blue macaws spend their whole life with the same partner and die of a broken heart when their mate disappears, Ana María lost her taste for living when she buried her husband. After the funeral, after all the battles fought and won, after living through a hundred years of democracies and dictatorships, republics and revolts, an oil boom and a coup d'état, she realized she had reached the limits of her body with the same speed as those of her century. The world was even madder than when she had suggested to Antonio that they retire under the pergola during the dictatorship. She shut herself in her room, giving as a pretext that no one needed her anymore since everybody had left the house on Avenida 3H, plugged in a landline telephone that she planted in the middle of her bed, lay her head down on four pillows, and never left it until the day she was put in her coffin.

No one ever saw her again, no one knew what became of the first woman doctor of Zulia at the end of her life. In the following six years, new metro stations were inaugurated, the Sabaneta prison was set alight in an arson attack, the most beautiful woman in the world was crowned as Miss Universe, the pope traveled from the Vatican to bless the basilica of Nuestra Señora de Coromoto, the victims of the Cariaco earthquake and of the hostage crisis of Terrazas del Ávila were cremated, a solar eclipse plunged the country into total darkness, but throughout all these upheavals, Ana María did not leave her room. For six years, she had no known relationships with the outside world, until February 2, 1999, when she was brought out into the street in her four-poster bed, carried by six Indigenous men, the same day when it was announced on television that the young lieutenant with the red beret, who had failed in his coup d'état on February 4, 1992, had become the president of Venezuela.

He had spent two years in prison. Every day, no matter what the hour, people had come to visit, to bring him food, books, a refrigerator, and a stove, so that when he was released, a security cordon was required, for half the city had crowded around the building to see the most beloved convict of the country. He had founded a party, conducted a campaign, and on the day of the elections, voting papers had come in from the city center, the shacks and the shantytowns, from the military barracks and the middle classes searching for illusions, from all those hands that had applauded him as he was being dragged through the streets toward Yarc Prison.

Within a few months, institutions of popular power were created, micro-credit and cooperative banks were opened, school fees were canceled, a ministry for women's rights was set up, a new constitution was signed. The publishing houses were nationalized, so that a book could become cheaper than a bottle of water. On all the nightstands, even in the poorest households, the same classics and little poetry collections could be found, signed by renowned writers and picked up by chance in a bookshop. Debates were organized on topics of general interest, which during the entire previous history of the country had never taken place outside of intimate political circles. A steady stream of people went through the legislative palace, from district committees to ecological groups and human rights organizations. The debates were broadcast on television so that lawmaking was accessible to all.

Ana María observed this revolution with astonishment, as one that she had never thought possible in her lifetime. But old age prevented her from participating in it. In the half-light of her last home, she was nothing more than the shadow of what she had once been.

She spent her days in pajamas and a long robe with a pattern of white flowers. Her expression was morose, and only the neighbor Zina came to visit to prepare her meals for the week and polish her mirrors. Whenever Venezuela called her mother, their conversations would be punctuated by long silences, and she could sense the exhaustion in Ana María's bones pass through her voice. To listen to her, although she remained perfectly lucid until the last hour of her life, one would think that she was living in another era altogether, that she was moving through an atmosphere of withered memories and ancient loves, a languishing breath of air in which a smell of dust and barbiturates still lingered. As an old lady now, what she had left behind had become more noble and more desirable than what she was presently experiencing, but the jungles of time forbade her from returning to that lost sweetness, and she knew she could expect nothing more from the past.

When Venezuela announced that Cristóbal had decided to live in Maracaibo, Ana María did not understand.

"There is nothing to see in this house," she said, "except for a very old woman dying very slowly."

"He wants to write novels," Venezuela replied. "What can I say?"

"Why?"

"Who knows?"

Reclining like a lioness, her head supported by a mountain of pillows, enthroned in her home like a duchess, Ana María paid no attention to that announcement, and after a long silence, remembered the day when Antonio had laid the notebook with a thousand love stories in her lap.

"I always thought I would die before him," she answered.

This was the situation Cristóbal found when he arrived in the house on Avenida 3H. He was then a young man of eighteen, short, with a fixed expression of permanent surprise, very dark brown hair that curled in the humidity, and with a nose that fell heavily over graceless lips. No one knew exactly how he had got there. He wore a Borsalino with a narrow rim and a rough canvas jacket, an old-fashioned item he had found in a thrift store in Paris.

People later said that he had been seen strolling the neighborhood with the air of a tourist, walking through the stifling streets, naively looking up at the majestic homes dating back to the oil boom, searching for clues in the painted arcades of the porches, trying to find in his childhood memories the entrance to his family home.

Only Zina, the neighbor, who had known all the generations of the Borjas Romeros, and who had not lost the habit of sitting under her awning and contemplating the world going by, observed him lost in the middle of the sidewalk and found him to look so much like Antonio that she believed he had been resurrected from the dead.

"If you didn't look so much like your grandfather," she cried, "I would say you were a French producer."

She led him to the mirrored bedroom where Ana María was living as a recluse. He entered slowly. The first time she saw him, wearing his hat and little Sorbonne student glasses, with his leather shoes and bohemian jacket, she thought he had come straight out of a Baudelaire poem, and was convinced that this garb was the symbol of the ills of the century that the greatest European doctors had not been able to cure.

"If you go out dressed like that," she said, "you'll get locked up."

"This is how French writers dress."

She was silent for a long time as she examined him from head to foot.

"Your mother left this house to go to Paris. Now you've left Paris to come here. I don't understand a thing anymore."

Cristóbal, who had followed his instincts, was the one who understood the least. All he knew was that in his house in the suburbs of Paris, he had imagined the Caribbean with the same passion as his mother, thirty years earlier, had imagined Europe. He could also see himself setting out for that world that was as changeable as the sea, where the villages gravitated around the cities like planets around stars, and where simple rain showers could awaken volcanoes. All he knew was that his reading had inspired him to travel there and that his heart was shivering with the desire to explore the country, as if his ancestors were still expressing themselves through the words on those pages.

To begin with, he was hesitant about setting out, but the idea gradually became a reality. At first mad and reckless, it became plausible and interesting, then attractive but perilous, then fascinating and overpowering, and what had started out as willful blindness was transformed into an obsession. He decided to head for the house on Avenida 3H, on the other side of the Atlantic, little suspecting what awaited him there, under the sun of what was called the revolution, a world of dangers and disasters, of disillusionment and flames, a world where all that remained of the myths were the ruins of exhaustion.

Cristóbal and Ana María got used to living together, not so much as grandson and grandmother but as two strangers. It took Cristóbal a long time to get used to his new life, in this new city, so different from the protected and harmonious world he had come from. He settled into the room next door to the one with mirrors, the same room in which Pedro Clavel had hung his hammock one night, and set up his French library there by having his books shipped from Paris. The first few days, Cristóbal would just sit in the garden, starting the first pages of novels or drafts of writing projects, looking around with his distracted air for spectacular scenes as if he could see them floating between the monstera leaves. Nothing awakened his interest except for the reading that fueled his imagination.

For several days, it was impossible to get him out of the house, convinced as he was that inspiration could be found only between the pages of books. Nobody, not even those who had never written a single line, could understand how anyone could aspire to create a novel without spending time in the noisy community of men and women, without getting mired in the same clay as them, understanding their stories, eating their meals, sitting at their tables, until the day when Ana María called Cristóbal into her room and said these words to him: "If you want to become a writer, talk to the people who aren't."

In those days, the government had decided to create an agrarian reform by reclaiming land deemed unproductive and giving it back to the people. The Venezuelan government had taken control of almost three million hectares of arable land and formed more than twenty thousand farming cooperatives. Thanks to Don Victor Emiro Montero, Cristóbal was able to find a position and enrolled in this program of expropriations.

He joined a team of revolutionaries whose mission was to take back the land from the latifundistas and to give it to the farmers at no cost. Cristóbal, who knew nothing about the market economy, dove in headfirst, not so much to save the world but to cultivate his imagination. Little did he know that what he experienced in that period of his life would be forever branded in his memory, so that many years later, when he returned to Paris, his mind full of torment and doubt, he could not erase the intensity of those first impressions.

Cristóbal was enrolled in a kind of expropriation brigade. He was sent to Maracay. The task was to buy back the fields belonging to an ancient clan of landowners, the Pistolettos, who owned a magnolia plantation. The Pistolettos were a family of twelve siblings whose origins were in Sardinia. All the brothers were born and had grown up in the Serbariu mine, in the middle of the Mediterranean. Their lungs had been reduced to dust, when famine, delinquency, and sickness had compelled the youngest, Carmilino Pistoletto, to flee that dark and violent region where coal dust seeped from the linen in the babies' cradles and the very fabric of dreams, so toxic that it had carried off every member of the generation before his by the age of thirty. He left the bowels of the Sardinian earth, convinced that he could foresee his own death, his mind ablaze with legends of a land of plenty where charcoal was used only to make people's skin gleam, and boarded a vessel registered in Malta carrying immigrants from every frontier—Jews and Arabs, Protestants and Christians—all piled up in the bottom of the hold, who prayed during the storms in a collective murmur of four different languages. Among them was an old exiled Moldavian man who owned a plant nursery. His pockets were filled with magnolia seeds.

"Flowers are for women," Carmilino had said.

"Flowers," the Moldavian had replied, "are money."

Carmilino Pistoletto swapped the seeds for some dried salami, disembarked in Venezuela, found some abandoned land where nobody had sown anything for a thousand years, planted the magnolia seeds, and a few months later, flavored all the sorbets, all the custards, all the jellies, all the liqueurs, turning those miraculous magnolias into an essential culinary ingredient. Having become a rich man, stimulated by his blossoming success, he had a large house built on the sweltering hot plain where he lived with his new family. All around the mansion, he built shacks and bunkhouses with beaten-earth walls and rusty corrugated tin roofs, where the peasants who started working for him lived.

The men planted the flowers, maintained the garden, did the grafting. The women did the repotting, cutting, isolating, pruning, while the Pistoletto family paid them a fixed salary and took a margin on resale. Four generations of Pistolettos followed one another in this home, far from the mines and the coal dust of Sardinia, far from the island famine and the cruelty that poverty begets, reproducing the same feudal system they had escaped five thousand miles away.

It had been such a long time since anyone had contested this pyramid of servitude and domination that everybody was surprised, one fine morning in September, to see the emissaries of the revolution appear after a journey from the capital. They showed up on the Pistoletto property with a warrant of expropriation and announced that they had come to buy the land, to claim the flowers, which from now on belonged to the people, and to support the farmers in founding a cooperative. The granddaughter of Carmilino Pistoletto, a woman in her forties with square hands, wide hips, and a well-tempered character, who had kept the anger of Sardinian families in her blood, barely took the time to greet them and banged her fist on the table.

"I don't want any thieves here!"

The argument brought the peasants out of their shacks. That was when Cristóbal first saw them. Their clothes were in tatters, their eyebrows bushy, their hair long, their feet filthy, everything about them in stark contrast to the luxury of the Pistoletto family's residence. Attracted by the comings and goings of the government cars and the negotiations, they stood silently under the trees, waiting for the verdict, or sat down on the roots and the fallen boughs, contemplating this scene without really understanding it.

"The land belongs to those who work it," said a man with a face furrowed by labor. "That's what Marx says, apparently."

"Who's Marx?" asked another peasant.

"It must be one of those gentlemen talking with Pistoletto."

After interminable debates, lengthy equivocations, and discussions that made old Carmilino roll over in his grave, a price for compensation was agreed upon. Against their will, muttering insults through their teeth, the Pistoletto family signed the seizure documents, and the next minute, the fields of magnolias, which had once made the fortune of a poor miner's son from Sardinia, were in the hands of the revolution.

A new farmers collective was organized, as agreed. Resources were pooled, groups were created, costs were reduced, and tasks were allocated. So many new words were spoken during this labor redistribution that the farmers felt like they were being taught not only how to work all over again but also a new language.

Cristóbal spent a week with them in one of the shacks surrounding the field. Although it was dilapidated, its walls were skillfully decorated with family photographs and the cracks in the plaster were hidden behind hanging scarves. The furniture, picked up secondhand in the village junk stores, was only a rummage of handmade constructions made of kapok wood, set down here and there with genteel attention, with embroidered cloths and ebony crucifixes displayed on them. The separation of the sleeping areas was created by simple curtains with colored patterns, held up on strings, behind which one could catch a glimpse of bunk beds and mattresses on the floor. Everything was clean, tidy, and carefully maintained. And in that kingdom of penury where a discreet harmony had endowed all things with order, it was never necessary to set out vases of flowers, for the scent of thousands of magnolias blooming outside would invade the rooms every day with the force of a deluge.

Cristóbal and the four peasant families signed the new ownership papers. They opened a bottle of cocuy, a liqueur made from leaves and plants by one of the daughters, a beautiful tall mixed-race woman with a wasp waist whose very short hair covered her round head like moss on a pebble. Her name was Fauna.

Their eyes met and Cristóbal was gripped with a blend of softness and desire. She had fine skin, delicate fingers, and an obvious penchant for reverie. The years of labor hunched over the flowers in the magnolia fields had not subdued her voluptuous curves or the innocence in her eyes. Cristóbal knew that he would see her again.

Three months later, the government sent the same team to the property to follow up on the reform. Cristóbal was one of them. When he arrived, he was astonished to see the state of abandonment of the fields, which were covered in weeds and brambles. He found the peasants sitting with their arms crossed. He asked, "Why have you not been working the land? It belongs to you now."

"Because Pistoletto left with the tractors," a man replied.

The government bought tractors from China, brand new, flame red, straight from an Asian factory. As soon as they arrived on those tropical lands, the news spread to all the surrounding villages and very quickly the plantation was overrun with children with dirty hair in shorts and sandals, women carrying babies in shawls, and men with shovels over their shoulders, all hastily called from their pastures to come see the machines that the revolution had acquired from thousands of miles away. A pastor from a neighboring parish was even brought out and, gasping for breath after walking along the road under the sun, he sprinkled the machines' wheels with holy water, and that very evening, in the now empty home of the ancient Pistoletto family, he presided over a peasant fiesta with guitars and singing, prayers and litanies, seized with such intense emotion that he appeared to be celebrating the invention of a new religion.

Cristóbal participated in the festivities. In the middle of the night, as he was getting ready to leave the fields and return to Maracaibo, Fauna pulled him into a small building. It was a kind of shed on the side of the field, which was used for the enfleurage of the magnolias, where there was a jumble of glass plates covered in petals and carboys of tallow, which the Pistoletto family had acquired in the hopes of setting up a perfume business. The room, where the fragrance of the flower buds was captured, had a heady smell of alcohol.

Plunged into darkness, Cristóbal felt cold lips seeking his face. Fauna undressed him, explored his skin, bit his neck, unbuttoned his pants, gobbled him up in a flood of kisses, and he felt as if he were one of the flowers freshly picked and being pressed to extract its oil. A palpitating tumult coursed through him to the roots of his hair, an internal cataclysm of which he had never before explored the amplitude, for only love leads back to the beginning of the world and to the memory of men. Although he knew nothing of this woman whom he had so recently met, he had the feeling that this scene was repeating itself in an infinite loop, as if the assault of Leona Coralina on Antonio, so long ago, was exhuming a message from the past within him. A footstep had been pressed into the sands of nostalgia and he soon knew that those clandestine loves would be the only ones that his memory would never allow him to forget.

When she was finished with him, Fauna hastily got dressed, left the shack without a word, and Cristóbal was certain that he would remember this instant with its flowery smell of alcohol for years, when that young mixed-race woman with her short hair and divine skin had expropriated him from his own body just as he had done with her lands.

Three months later, when he came back to follow up on the work, nothing had moved. The tractors, standing in the middle of the fields like statues, covered in dust and mud, immobile and silent, had not been turned on since the day they arrived.

"Why have you not worked the land?" Cristóbal asked.

"Because the tractors are in Chinese. And we don't understand Chinese."

A delegation of engineers was brought from China to Venezuela specially to translate the ideograms on the dashboard, as if they were oracular inscriptions engraved on the shell of a turtle from the Zhou dynasty. One Tuesday morning at nine, while the farmers were still in their shacks, they heard the sound of a government convoy, a caravan of cars heading their way from over the horizon, just a few minutes after a child burst into the room shouting, "The Chinese are coming!"

The delegation from Hong Kong stayed for a week. A crowd of onlookers formed around them to listen to them speak their language with its extraordinary sounds, and followed them in all their movements in order to re-create the same prophetic and skillful gestures, which must have raised the greatest wall in the world. When they left, the peasants continued to execute those same gestures, with the same slowness and devotion, as if the tractors could be set in motion only by the mystery of this magic.

The next time Cristóbal returned, he could not believe his eyes. Years later, he would still be incapable of recalling that scene without being astonished, dumbfounded. When he arrived in the magnolia fields, he found the tractors working, the flowers open and blooming, but it only took him a few minutes to realize that one of the families, larger than the others, had taken possession of the Pistoletto home and paid the three others a salary to take care of the magnolia plantation. The farmers had reproduced exactly what they had hoped to overcome.

It was perhaps this event, although an insignificant one overall, that made the first fractures of the revolution apparent to Cristóbal. He noted the profound economic failings, the insecurity and shortages, the beginnings of a massive exile, the unstoppable inflation that led to prices multiplying by three from one week to the next. On the east side of the city, in the middle-class neighborhoods, the demonstrations never stopped, to the rhythm of banging on pots and pans.

The country was divided. There was talk of abandoned investments, of the flight of financial oligarchies, of the isolation in which the country now found itself. The revolution was nothing more than a "dictatorship in disguise." Devaluation was inevitable. In the space of fifteen years, the national currency suffered three reconversions, which made it lose fourteen zeros. Throughout the country, every day at the same time, hundreds of men and women would say a collective prayer against tyranny. Before 8:00 a.m., in the gardens and on the terraces, in every lost village, on every island off the coast, in the countryside and on the beaches, in the hospitals and the cars in the middle of traffic jams, all those who opposed the current government held a great vigil, to gather their forces and send that lieutenant with the red beret back to the prison he never should have left.

This was the source of a rift that would soon lead the country into a profound crisis, as Cristóbal foresaw after the scene with the tractors, when he returned to the house on Avenida 3H with a surly expression, a worried mind, and a downtrodden mood. In his white hammock in the back courtyard, protected by the bougainvillea vines that Eva Rosa used to water and by the scent of the carnations that once crowned the head of the child Pedro Clavel, Cristóbal was overcome by sadness. He had not seen King Solomon's mines nor the cities of Paititi, and what he had thought might become a new world turned out to be nothing but a chimera. He could not find the rest that he had been looking forward to for so long, and the only idea that persisted in him was that all that triumphs is doomed to failure. He spoke about this to Ana María, who still had not left her four-poster bed, lying with her telephone in the middle of the sheets. She replied that she had spent her whole life waiting for that moment only to discover that tigers had been replaced by tigers.

"The people are exhausted," she said. "Corruption will eat away at this project."

Cristóbal said nothing. For his idealistic spirit, corruption was an anonymous, faceless phantom, a rotten apple that grew only on the tree of capitalism, and a blight that affected only populations that had sold their souls to the devil, as if it were a punishment for their greed. Never had the thought so much as crossed his mind that corruption might be growing right there beside him, in the moist soil of revolutions, a daughter of excess nurtured by those who fought it, in the very offices where its destruction was professed, in the mouths of the most progressive leaders. He had never imagined that it might be standing in line at the supermarket, drinking a beer in a bar, going to the swimming pool, exercising, taking the children to day care, making love. He could not imagine that corruption was not just the feature of imperialist regimes but that it was everywhere. Revolutions drank at its wells too. They failed because people forgot to do what had kindled them in order to fuel them.

In a world that was changing at incredible speed, Ana María and Cristóbal supported each other with the trust of old soldiers, brought together in the complicity of their new life, counting on the love that they were gradually discovering. Zina visited them on rainy days, wearing a paisley shawl over her head. Seeing Cristóbal frenetically editing his aborted manuscripts, his beginnings of novels, she could not refrain from asking him, "What are you writing?"

"I don't know. A novel about Maracaibo, I think."

She remained silent.

"I know nothing about novels," she said after a moment. "But I do know that the peasants of Maracaibo are convinced that in every litter of kittens there is a jaguar. The prudent mother cat isolates it, chases it away, to stop it from devouring the other kittens. It grows up differently. It emancipates itself. Those are the builders of this city. We are all the sons of a dream of a jaguar."

She fell silent again. She remembered her French producer and the thousands of love stories she would have liked to act in.

"Promise me that one day, it will be a movie. Promise me that one day, you will make us into stars."

Two weeks went by. One Tuesday in November, Cristóbal came to kiss his grandmother's forehead before going to work and was troubled by the sight of a shadow on her face. He was not able to find the vivacity, the sparkling glow that he was used to seeing in it, for her eyes seemed darker, as if the petals of a thousand fields of magnolias had withered under her eyelids. Ana María did her best to let nothing show, but only she knew the reason for this. That morning, she had seen the moth in her room. She had caught sight of it for the first time at dawn, as it was flitting between the blades of her ceiling fan, and then again shortly after her breakfast, and she recognized it immediately.

It was the same black *tara* that had announced Chinco's death, the same giant moth that had appeared to her in dreams, and there was nothing terrifying about it, apart from the fact that it had come too soon. To begin with, she saw it as an early sign of the end and thought it was an advance greeting from the great beyond. She did not want to pay attention to this symbol of death, and continued to live normally, with a few more precautions and more defiance, such that she eventually told herself that the *tara* was no more than a flight of fancy.

But this evil omen was not a mirage. The next day, at dawn, before she woke up, she had a strange dream about a man who was having difficulties carrying another man on his shoulders, in which the cries of newborn babies blended with the gunshots from the arquebus of Pedro Maldonado, soldiers' heavy boots, and the beating of drumrolls, and all those confused images led her to understand that it was not just a nightmare that was drawing to a close but also the life that she had lived until then. She opened her eyes one last time and saw, in a corner of the ceiling, resting between its enormous wings, the black *tara* waiting for her.

At around seven that evening, when Cristóbal came home from work, he went into Ana María's room and found her motionless, her head resting on her four pillows, a smile on her lips, her eyes masked by a veil with which she had taken the trouble of covering her face. She lay, perfumed and beautiful, dressed in the long silk robe that she had worn half a century earlier for the delivery of her daughter, with two blazing candles standing vigil on either side of her. He knelt in front of his grandmother, and on seeing her combed hair, her childlike expression, her closed eyes, the medals of the Virgin on her chest, he wanted to cry, but couldn't.

She was buried in a plot in the heart of the El Cuadrado cemetery, next to Antonio. Two hundred unknown anonymous women, whom no one had ever seen before, attended the ceremony, and everyone understood that their lives must have been saved by Ana María at one time. Of all the friends who were present, it was the male nurses of the maternity clinic, wearing their white coats, who carried the coffin from the church to the tomb. During the service, Cristóbal observed the scene with wide round eyes, and the sad melodies that were played, the Scriptures read by the priest who came to bless her departure, the incense that filled the cemetery with its fragrance all seemed to be a celestial lament. Three days later, he received a letter of condolence from the president of the republic, which spoke of the duty of memory and of great women, but no one opened it.

That is how nothing was left of that woman with piercing eyes and lively intelligence except that cold tomb, an extinguished glory, and a few words that were engraved on her tombstone, thus fulfilling a prophecy she had uttered herself, the day she had met Lya Imber de Coronil:

Here lies Ana María Rodríguez
The first woman doctor.

Venezuela attended the funeral, after a hasty return. Her pain was such that she did not speak for three days. Along with Cristóbal, she emptied Ana María's room. They detached the mirrors from the walls and sold them as relics of the past, unscrewed the feet of the bed, took out the lamps that no one had lit for years, and unhooked the heavy muslin curtains, which then let so much light into the room that lost objects from the time of Eva Rosa were found. Floundering up to their eyes in a swamp of carpets and packing boxes, they turned the whole room inside out, and after moving the four-poster bed and the hundreds of medical books Ana María had collected since her student days in Caracas, they washed the walls of the room with so much energy that the neighborhood woke up in the middle of the siesta thinking that a new oil well had been discovered in the middle of the garden.

The last day, Cristóbal remembered the story that Ana María had told him, before her departure, about the funeral of her own father. He suspected that his grandmother had also hidden a secret treasure in her room. He tapped along all the baseboards, just as she had done long ago at Chinco's death, and discovered a little coffer behind a hollow board. It was shaped like a trunk with a curved lid and gave off a scent of violets. Inside it he found a brown package, tied with butcher's string, like the kind used for tying up pieces of meat. In his solitude, relieved of all weight, Cristóbal untied the string, opened the package, and found an old school notebook that seemed to have survived the mold and termites.

It was the notebook of a thousand love stories that Antonio had transcribed many years ago in the central bus station of Maracaibo. Cristóbal spent the morning reading them, leafing through the pages, following the course of those thousand stories set down pell-mell in a prodigious disorder, whose sources had dried up, with the strange and contagious pleasure of reading something without really understanding it. He grew accustomed to the presence of these strangers, to the distant hubbub of that bus station where the young Antonio had sat down in the humble hope of deciphering love, their names jumbled in his head like a celebration, so that after an hour that anonymous multitude was no more than a single person. When he came to the last story, his heart was filled with red roses, in the same outpouring that had brimmed over his grandfather's head eighty years earlier, and it was just as he was closing the notebook that he noticed that there were still a few empty pages.

Then Cristóbal wanted to write his own. But his love story was not that of a man for a woman but that of a man for a country. Speaking about the world he had heard. Talking about what he had seen in the night of the birds of Maracaibo. Retaining the traces in the air. There had to be something left of those stories other than words, fleeting sentences passed down from generation to generation, from mouth to mouth, something besides gold brooches and shattered memories.

Where to start? From the miraculous encounter of a tropical princess with a political prisoner? Or should he haul himself back even further? Navigate through the sap of a family tree as one sails up the river of the past? Turn back in his tracks and pass through that stifling evening when Ana María delivered a daughter into the crowd of history, the day when a dictator was expelled from the country, and her cries blended with the cries of the streets? He needed to go back even further. To continue to dig. To find the book's bedrock. To tell the story of the statue of Simón Bolívar that once landed in the port of Santa Rita, and of the clandestine love affair of Eva Rosa, who survived the shot from the arquebus of Pedro Maldonado. To conjure up the giant moth that came to find Chinco at his death and the uncanny discovery of the penguin that washed up on the coast of Sinamaica one morning then became a jewel. He needed to explain the notebook with its thousand love stories from the central bus station and the procession of San Benito that had stopped the gusher of oil. He needed to go back even further. To describe the unreal landscapes of Pela el Ojo and the discreet dignity of Mute Teresa. To climb the hill of dreams. To drink from the roots.

Cristóbal took up a pen and started writing. He had to go all the way back to that morning when, on the third day of his life, Antonio Borjas Romero was abandoned on the steps of a church in a street that today bears his name.

About the Author

Miguel Bonnefoy was born in France in 1986 to a Venezuelan mother and a Chilean father. Two of his earlier novels, *Octavio's Journey* and *Black Sugar*, have sold more than thirty thousand copies each in France and have been translated into several languages. In 2013 Bonnefoy was awarded the Prix du Jeune Écrivain. His novel *Heritage* (Other Press, 2022) received widespread critical acclaim in France, including being short-listed for the Prix Femina, the Grand Prix de l'Académie française, and the Goncourt Prize. In 2024 *The Dream of the Jaguar* won the Grand Prix du roman de l'Académie française.

About the Translator

Ruth Diver holds a PhD in French and comparative literature from the University of Paris 8 and the University of Auckland, New Zealand. She won two 2018 French Voices Awards for her translations of *Marx and the Doll* by Maryam Madjidi, and *Titus Did Not Love Berenice* by Nathalie Azoulai. She also won *Asymptote*'s 2016 Close Approximations fiction prize for her translation of extracts of *Maraudes* by Sophie Pujas.